Mouse Trap

Bobby 'KING-B' Bowen

Cadmus Publishing
www.cadmuspublishing.com

DEDICATION

I dedicate this book to: Taniala, Tanara, Bobby Jr., Dream, Rayana, and Emone. Anytime I have ever felt "trapped", it was thinking of all of you that motivated me to "pull myself free". May you never be trapped in ways that I have.
  -Love Dad

Table of Contents

Chapter 1: Freedom

He jumped from the top bunk with a thud. His 6'2", 215 pound frame caused the slim redheaded white guy at the bottom bunk to sit up. He tied on his New Balance shoes and grabbed the white state shirt he'd been using as a pillow and threw it over his hand sewn wife beater.

"Damn, you fuckin' ripped dude! What do you do, workout every day?" the guy asked.

He wasn't much for small talk so he just smiled and nodded his head as he walked over to the metal pisser to piss, hopefully for his last time in prison.

The gym was dimly lit. It was a musty smelling area from lack of adequate cleaning. There were no bouncy new basketballs rolling around or a volleyball net running across the court. No, a guard stood overhead in a walk-cage with a gas gun watching everything, and a rusty universal weight set sat over in the corner.

The gym was packed with forty guys arranged in two groups of twenty and four rows of five.

"When I call your name," Beady-Eyes said, "stand up and say your name and number then sit your ass back down."

Beady-Eyes was one of those guards who brought all his free-world issues to work with him and got a sense of power back by lording over and talking down to others.

He was so close, yet so far away from his freedom. He imagined what he was feeling was something like a pro football player would on the receiving team right before the kickoff in the Super Bowl. The thud in his heart was a kick drum at a rock concert. Where would he go first after ten million plus minutes of incarceration? How long would it take him to regain his rhythm, his flow of free society?

He had lost contact with his only family years ago and so his plan was to get on the Greyhound bus and get off wherever his spirit said to get off.

"Ty Magnum." Hearing his name drew him from his thoughts. "54-31-30," he said after clearing the knot from his throat. He was in the second group, third person on the first row. "Magnum, you may be seated."

Mag sat and from the side of his right eye he could see the last person on the second row staring at him in an intense manner. This was a focused stare that sent alarms going off in Magnum's head.

"Juan Torrez," Beady-Eyes called out. The guy stood and Magnum took the opportunity to look directly at him.

Juan was dark and hard from many years in prison. The scar running down the length of his left arm was testimony of a past party with a sharp prison razor or a smuggled in box cutter. He was about 5'9" and 210 pounds. His eyes said that he wasn't a pushover by far. Magnum guessed he was in his mid-fifties but still had his raw strength.

"44-81-40," Magnum heard Torrez call out.

'At least a thirty year vet,' Magnum analyzed from the guy's number, 'What possible beef could he have with me?' Torrez sat down as the guard continued to call out names. Magnum continued to watch him.

Magnum felt his body tense up, the kick drum in his chest working overtime. He looked back and to his right. They locked eyes. Most people broke eye contact to show there was no problem, it was an unwritten rule, but not this guy. He clearly had something on his mind. His eyes spoke loud and clear and said, 'I've hurt many people with no mercy and you are next on my list.'

Magnum was perplexed. What possible issue could this man have with him? He shook his head. He didn't need this shit on the very day he was to regain his freedom.

"Stand to your feet," was shouted just before Magnum was about to ask school what his issue was. "Pair it up," Mr. Beady-Eyes shouted. The first group merged with the second group forming twenty pairs of two. Magnum was in the right hand line and three pairs from the middle of the line. His current problem was also in the right handed line but at the very end furthest from Beady-Eyes whom was leading the line.

Magnum knew that sometimes people get so used to living behind bars, having three hots and a cot, free laundry, a structured schedule to follow, that when it's time for them to leave the mental comforts of prison they have become dependent on, they snap and find a reason to get in trouble and stay.

It reminded Magnum of the old man in the movie SHAW-SHANK REDEMPTION, Brooks Hatlen "Maybe that's what's wrong with this school," Magnum thought. He was positive they hadn't crossed paths.

A light sweat had formed on Magnum's forehead. He stretched and pulled his muscles in order to loosen the tension that had moved in on his body. He was so close to his long awaited freedom, but yet still so far away. Like 2-Pac had said in one of his songs, his next moves had to be calculated steps.

The guy paired up next to him was rubbing his hands together like he was cold and since it wasn't cold Magnum chalked it up as excitement.

"This is it man. We almost out bro. Last step before I put that pound game down on baby ass. She in trouble!" Mag just nodded with a slight smile but was busy with his own personal excitement coupled up inside a dilemma. Any other day and this issue would have been handled quick, fast, and in a hurry; but a fight now could ruin everything, and wisdom and tact had to be his companions at this moment. In prison, assaulting a man over fifty is a free-world charge and Magnum was letting nothing get in the way of his freedom when he was so close. Nothing!

'Maybe if I just ignore the fool he'll focus his attention elsewhere. Maybe he's just crazy.' Magnum thought.

"Move out and follow me to the unit release processing building where you'll receive a social security card if you have one on file, a commissary check from the money on your books, clothes, and for the ones discharging you'll receive one hundred dollars, but only fifty for you all still on paper."

Magnum and the other men listened intently. Beady-eyes continued.

"After you are processed and everyone is finished, I'll release you to your families or to the busses. Do I make myself clear, fuckoids?"

"Yes, sir." they said. Magnum just shook his head.

"Then move the fuck out."

Magnum looked behind him. He knew for sure that Torrez had been at the very end of the line. He had moved up a pair and was just one pair behind him. Magnum had seen too many dudes get shanked from behind in prison hallways and chow hall lines to not stay alert at all times. Torrez was making his move, and Magnum knew he had to think quick.

The line was processing forward at a steady pace. Beady-eyes was leading the way, no guard in the rear. The release process building was fifteen or twenty feet away now. Magnum looked back and into Torrez's eyes, anger and determination. Magnum knew that he would make his move soon. A small pang of fear rippled through the pit of Magnum's stomach. Not fear of what Torrez might do to him, but fear of losing his long awaited second-chance at life. He had to get this moment right. He wasn't going back.

Adrenaline flooded his body, all five senses on high alert in survival mode.

They were ten feet away from the processing building when Torrez made his move. Magnum heard a quick shuffle of feet. His ears perked up.

"Hey dude, you're not cutting me in line." Magnum heard the guy right behind him say.

Magnum spun to his right with lightening speed just in time to see the light reflecting off of the flattened steel in Torrez's hand. Magnum used his momentum to crash his right elbow into the right side of Torrez's head. He immediately dropped the shank. The impact was a crushing blow, two hundred and fifteen pounds of solid force. Torrez was unconscious before he hit the ground.

Acting fast, thinking faster, Magnum put the shank Torrez tried to use against him into Torrez's sock and yelled, "Hey, this guys having a heat stroke! Call for help! Heat stroke! Hurry!" Magnum moved back into line. Beady-eyes ran back towards the commotion.

"What the hell is going on here?" Magnum said nothing.

"The old guy just started shaking and passed out." It was the redheaded slim white guy from earlier in his cell. He winked at Magnum and Magnum nodded his appreciation back.

Beady-eyes called the infirmary to come get Torrez. By the time he woke up, Magnum would be long gone.

CHAPTER 2: THE RELEASE

Right before entering the processing building, Magnum looked back and saw a stretcher carrying Torrez away. He breathed a sigh of relief and silently thanked his father, Tyson Magnum, for teaching him how to read body language at such a young age, and prison for giving him plenty of practice in sharpening those skills. His dad was a sharp man and would say, "Son, listen to what the mouth is saying, but watch the eyes and body for the truth." Magnum remembered one time his dad was interacting with a woman. Her words were telling his father that she was done with his lack of being exclusive and she didn't desire him in that way at all anymore. She wanted nothing to do with him. In a smooth and gentle way, his father told her okay and that he understood and walked off. Back in the car his dad said to him, "Son, did you see how she kept stroking her hair and the way her inner thighs kept opening and closing?" Mag nodded yes. "Her mouth was telling me that she no longer was satisfied with our sexual relationship without a commitment from me, but her body was telling me that she wants me to come back through later. Did you catch that son?" Mag nodded yes. "Always watch the body." Those earlier lessons saved Magnum's life on several occasions and he was thankful he'd paid attention.

The inmate release process building looked like a DMV building going out of business. Dull overhead light gave the room a sad feel for such an exciting moment. Magnum figured it was the prison's last attempt to depress you before it let you go. The place was tidy and the folding metal chairs were in four rows of ten. Magnum guessed right that this was the waiting area, for this is where Beady-eyes had them sit.

"When the lady calls your name, go up to the counter, get processed out, and come back to your seat." Beady-eyes said. They were processing each person out at about five minutes a person, five at a time.

The anticipation of being on his own, being responsible for every aspect of his life, had Magnum high with adrenaline. His heart rate had slowed but the party was still rocking in his chest. He unconsciously rubbed his elbow; A close call. His only real focus at the time: get out and travel the great state of Texas. No burdens, just freedom and life. He had once looked up the definition of freedom and he loved the one that had said, '(freedom from) not being affected by something undesirable.'

'Liberation, liberty, deliverance, self-government.' Magnum just wanted to get on the bus, stop where his heart told him to, and explore before he moved on to the next city or town; allow the spirit to lead and guide him.

"Ty Magnum." He heard his name called, blinked away his thoughts, and walked up to the counter where a heavy-set Caucasian lady awaited him. It was hard for Magnum not to notice her cleavage. It was as if she was advertising the perks of the awaiting free-world. She was looking down at her paperwork when Magnum approached the counter. "Can you please state your-" she looked up and paused in mid-sentence. She was looking at Magnum like a smoked turkey after a three day fast.

She said, "I don't mean to be forward, but you have very beautiful eyes, sir. What color are they?" She was fanning herself with her right hand like she was in heat. Her left hand was under the desk now. Magnum didn't even want to imagine what it was doing under there.

Magnum smiled shyly, then made a quick decision to be patient with the overweight woman with the double D's.

"Thank you. I get that a lot. They are light grey and hazel, and by the way, my number is 543130." Magnum said, trying not to seem too anxious to get the process moving along.

She looked down at the paperwork, "Wow. Nineteen years. I know you can't wait to slip into something, shall we say, warm and moist."

Magnum looked directly into her eyes, surprised by her forwardness. She was holding up his freedom and he was ready to go. On top of that, he was still in prison and an establishing a relationship case could possibly get him turned around.

Magnum tried to play the shy role by ignoring the comment and placing his ID card on the counter, "What else do you need from me, ma'am?"

Her eyes narrowed, "Don't ignore me Ty!" She said his name like she'd known him her whole life. "I can make this a very long drawn out process." Then she added, "Do you want to play games with me Ty?"

Magnum didn't speak right away. He focused and gave her a quick character analysis: no ring, late thirties, uses control and position to make up for her physical insecurities. Her attitude showed that she hated rejection and her forwardness told Magnum that she'd done this two-bit act before. She'd most likely met the freshly released inmates at the cheap hotel by the bus stop after work, picked them up, fed them, got her back beat in, and then sent them on their way with a smile. Fair exchange is no robbery.

From the book 'The Art of War' he'd learned that to make your opponent feel like they had the advantage was actually to your advantage. Magnum gave her his most seductive look, deep eye to eye contact, and leaned in a little.

"Baby, after nineteen years and no practice, I'm shy. I was thinking a woman of your caliber, as sexy as you are, I might not keep up. But now that you have challenged me, this is what we're going to do." Magnum leaned in and whispered the rest. She smiled, her face flushed, and she finished processing Magnum out. By the time she realized what was really going on, he'd be long gone. Magnum walked off, slightly shaking his head thinking, "The things we do for freedom."

After changing into the light grey jogging pants they'd issued him and the wife beater tank top, Magnum went back to his seat. His only possessions in the world at that time were his state inmate ID card that said 'Texas Inmate' in big blue and red letters, a hundred dollar TDCJ check, another check for the money from his books for twelve thousand eight hundred dollars, and a bus ticket.

In prison Magnum was big on doing his time versus passing it and he made sure that financial hustle was a part of his focus. Early in his sentence he had pulled some strings to get into the coveted craft shop where you could invest in leather, wood, and art supplies that you could turn around and sell to the guards or send home for your family to sell for you. Magnum had perfected his craft in leathers, purses, book cases, and wallets. Selling drugs in prison was never his thing and so he also heard that one could make a lot of money with the right job in the prison food service. Once in, Magnum made his way into a cook position and found a connect with an old-school cat named Squeak who worked in the butchers shop. Squeak would sell Magnum cases of meat at cheap prices and Magnum would sell the meat and make a huge profit that he had cash apped to a friend. The friend would then send the money to his books. Between the craft shop and the kitchen, he had done well for himself. In total he was now sitting on $12,900 to get him started.

The last two inmates were coming back from the exit processing counter smiling, an extra pep in their step. There was a nervous excitement in the room. The dude to Mag's left was biting his nails. Two dudes in front of him shook hands with smiles on their faces. The only sad thing about the entire situation was that out of the forty guys getting out that day, half would be back within a couple of years. Recidivism was a real problem in the prison system because prison is a place where a man has to intentionally change around the way he sees life and dig deep in soul searching to find the root causes of his patterns and behaviors. Many men lack this discipline and fall into the flow of the system and end up merely passing their time with television shows, board games, and drugs. It was sad, but the truth.

"Ok, dip-shits. It's time for you to get the hell out of my prison." Beady-eyes said. "I'll keep the bed warm for some of ya's. You'll come back to daddy. You always do."

Magnum felt a rush of excitement flood his spirit. He couldn't believe the moment he'd dreamed of for nineteen years was finally at hand. His plan was to get on the bus and ride until his spirit told him to get off; freedom. No real plans, just flow. No attachments. We make plans. Life has a way of trying to change them.

Chapter 3: Jasmine

The June 27th, 2023 sun was high in the sky as Magnum entered the grassy courtyard through the door labeled 'release'. He let the moment consume him as he inhaled the fresh morning air. With every inhale, he felt a vibration hum within his chest. It was almost overpowering. Finally, he was free! Able to go and do anything his heart desired. He walked off of the sidewalk leading into the parking lot and into the grass lot. He bent down and picked up a blade of grass and smelled it before he let it flow through his fingers. Freedom was like no other smell in the world. Magnum smiled. His body not only felt free, but his mind felt liberated from the stress and longing that comes from doing time. The days and nights of being looked down on and identified as just a number in a system, and being surrounded by not only the dark energy of prison but the manifestations that the darkness bred, Magnum knew that these concepts existed in society but with his freedom he wasn't trapped in it.

He looked up into the endless Texas sky in Huntsville as tears of joy flowed over the edge of his eyes. He outstretched his long arms to the side, head back and up, and whispered, "Thank you." Magnum wasn't a very religious man, but deeply believed in relationship with the creator. He knew that God was as real as the free air he was now breathing and knew on a deeper level that God's grace is why he was standing there. He had to have respect for anyone who could create the heavens and earth with just spoken words, set the sun just the right distance from the earth so that it wouldn't burn up or freeze out. What truly amazed Magnum is how everything in the world was interconnected in small but intricate ways. We wouldn't be able to even breathe without the trees and the dung from the cows is what naturally fertilizes the plants. Magnum was in awe of the Big Man's knowledge, wisdom, and understanding.

The sound of laughter caused Magnum to drop his head and arms to focus on the scene before him. He blinked the tears away and dried his eyes with the back of his hand. The men with no family to pick them up were already halfway up the road, eager to get on the bus and get going towards their destination. Some were in cars already pulling off, ready to relish in their first taste of free world food, others pulling off eager to get their first taste of baby in the back seat in a parking lot down the road. Everyone seemed happy.

A total contrast to the entire picture jumped out at Magnum from the right hand side of the parking lot. A beautiful Hispanic woman, maybe thirty three to thirty five years old, curly silk like black hair down her back, was crying, looking towards the door where all the inmates had come from. She was about 5'9", perfect long legs, stunning; Magnum couldn't take his eyes off of her.

She was about twenty feet away, leaning back on a cream colored BMW. She was dressed casual in short white designer shorts and gold heels that made the length of her legs run for miles.

The halter top shirt showed off her flat and toned stomach. She carried her age in a sophisticated manner, very classy and not attempting to appear too young like a lot of the older female guards Magnum had encountered in prison, with their caked-on makeup and tight uniforms. This lady was stunning, and with little effort.

She seemed to be looking directly at Magnum now. He looked behind him, no one there. He looked back. She waved him over in a way that said "I really need help". Before he made a conscious decision his legs were already taking him in her direction, half the reason being that he was wired to help those in need, the other half not so humanitarian. 'What are you doing?' His mind asked him. He smiled to himself when the first line of bump and grind came to mind: 'My minds telling me no, but my body, my body is telling me yes.'

The closer he got, she became that much more beautiful. The high Indian cheek bones in her face reminded him of Salena. Those big round walnut colored eyes put Sophia V's to shame. Tears lined her smooth brown cheeks.

Magnum was arms length away now. They locked eyes. He felt the blood rush through his manhood. He willed it not to rise, wasn't the time. If he wasn't mistaken, he could have sworn he saw the subtle hardening of her nipples through the light fabric of her shirt. He didn't want to risk looking directly at them. Maybe he had just been locked up too long. Magnum cleared his throat, but she spoke first.

"I apologize if I've interrupted your joyous moment of freedom, but I really need help." She kept glancing down at Magnum's chest, he noticed. She couldn't help it.

"It would take more than a few beautiful tears to steal my joy. Tell me what I can do to help or at least make you feel better." Magnum prided himself on his ability to help others find solutions to their issues. He gave her all his attention.

A powerful whiff of her perfume hit Magnum before she answered his question. He had to refocus.

"Umm," she began with a light accent, "I was waiting on my Uncle Torrez. I thought he was coming home today and I just got a call from the warden saying a shank that was found in his sock!" Tears were running wind-sprints down her face now. "What am I going to do? I drove all the way here from San Antonio." Her voice cracked and she leaned forward with her head on Magnum's chest.

It had been nineteen years since a woman's head had been on his chest. His mind was pulled in so many directions, but he focused.

"Calm down. Calm down beautiful." He felt conflicted knowing that he was the one who had inadvertently caused her anguish. Her hair smelled of watermelon kiwi. He was stroking it with his right hand, telling her to calm down.

"Look at me and listen." Magnum said. He quickly remembered that women are not always focused on the solution to the issue. They want to be heard, understood, and comforted most times.

Magnum looked deep in her eyes and spoke smooth and slow, "I can see and feel your pain, beautiful." He was looking into her soul through her eyes. "Driving all the way from SananTone, excited to see your Uncle, I can tell you love him a lot. Am I right . . . ?" He made the motion for her to fill in her name.

"Oh, Jasmine, Jasmine Cruz, sorry, what's yours?" She asked.

"You can just call me Mag. Everyone else does. See Jasmine, the ultimate measure of a woman is not where she stands in moments of comfort and convenience, but where she stands at times of challenge and controversy. Are you going to choose to stand on faith that this trial happened to develop a certain part of your character, or do you choose to embrace the sadness that comes with looking at this as a waste of your time?"

Mag stopped to let what he had just spoken soak in. While she contemplated his question, the way she looked into his eyes had a hungry nature to it, a deep dependence.

Mag continued, "Faith is taking the first step, even when you don't see the rest of the stair case. I know you're asking yourself how this minor setback could possibly help you and I can't give you a definitive answer, but in order to get the lesson, you must step out on faith that this moment is divine and has a purpose."

She seemed lost in the cadence of his words. They flowed off of his tongue like poetry. She nodded her head and dried her tears with the back of her thumb.

Mag felt the moment called for a hug. He pulled her in close. She wrapped her arms around. He let go and asked, "You going to be alright?"

"Yes, yes." she sniffled, "This is only going to make me stronger, and now that I think about it I do believe this moment is divine and was meant." Her eye contact lingered and she was biting her bottom lip.

Mag smiled, hugged her again, and began to walk off towards the bus station, not knowing how long he had to catch it.

He was about three feet away when he heard her call his name. She took a few tentative steps in his direction and asked, "So where you headed?"

Mag inhaled the cool morning air into his lungs, spread his arms, exhaled, and yelled, "Wherever I want to go!" He spun in a full circle with a big smile on his face. "I'm headed to explore this great state. I'm going to hop on the bus and ride until my spirit tells me to get off, explore that city or small town, connect with good people, and then it's on to the next. No plans, no commitments, just freedom."

"I like your name. It's strong." She said. "That's a beautiful dream you have too, just to roam free, exploring Texas. I admire that Magnum."

Mag frowned, "I don't remember telling you my full name. Did I?"

"Umm, yeah. You said that your name was Magnum but just to call you Mag. What? Do you think I'm a psychic or something?" She had inched closer and her hand was on his chest as she spoke and looked into his eyes.

"Or maybe you a stalker or something and you wanna taste some of this sweet chocolate at all cost." Mag looked right back into her eyes.

She said, "Why not let your first stop be the great city of San Antonio, the place that was key to building and establishing Texas as an independent state? Start where the state started. We have so much history there. A historical zoo that is over one hundred years old, countless historical restaurants, the River Walk, and the Alamo speaks for itself."

"Damn girl, you should be a tour guide or something." Mag could hear the hope in her voice, like she was holding her breath, that dependant look again. Something in his spirit was off but he couldn't put his finger on it. He ignored the feeling. He looked behind her towards her BMW gleaming in the morning sun, then looked over his shoulder towards the bus, towards his dream, his plan. He looked at the curve of her body, strong wide hips, the 'v' in her shorts had volume, perfect skin. Everything on his logic was telling him "get in the car stupid", but his spirit was telling him to stick to the script and follow his dream. He agreed.

He tried to be gentle, "What I will do is take your number down and when I slide through the Tone you will be the first person I ring. I appreciate the offer and everything, I really do, but I'm not trying to be a burden to anyone. I just want to stick to what my spirit is telling me and that's to stick to my plan."

She looked like the wind had been knocked out of her chest. Her hands were visibly shaking. The white parts of her eyes were instantly red. She was glaring at him. She stood like that for a second, then her head hit her hands and her shoulders began to heave.

"Hey, hey. Wait, don't cry. I didn't mean to offend you or nothing, it's just. Okay, okay, alright, calm down Jasmine. The least I can do is allow you to drop ya boy off in SanaTone, alright. You got a point. Why not start where it all started for Texas.

Mag was out of practice when it came to dealing with female tears and their emotional responses, especially since there was something instinctively inherent in his nature to make people feel better. Her shoulders stopped heaving. She was again wiping her face with her hands.

She looked up at him and smiled with mascara lightly smeared under her eyes, "You're going to love my city."

"Look Jasmine, I really appreciate the ride. When we get there, make sure I get that number so that we can at least chill a few times before I leave."

Her lips moved to the side of her face in a sarcastic manner as she grabbed his arm and lead him towards the beamer. Mag didn't object. Mag opened the driver's side door for her and closed it gently. He laughed to himself when he thought about taking off running. He was still smiling as he closed the passenger door on himself, but stopped as the feeling of a cell door closing rushed through his soul. He shook the feeling off.

"You okay?" she asked.

"Yeah, let's ride momma."

As she started the smooth powerful engine, Mag adjusted and slightly reclined his seat back for a more comfortable ride. He closed his eyes and thought about what he knew about the great city of San Antonio.

Chapter 4: San Antonio

A bump in the road caused Mag to open his eyes. Trying to dose off was useless. He was too excited and the country side reminded him of a country song called 'Fly Over States'.

After fumbling with the buttons on the side of the seat, Mag finally had the seat at the perfect angle where he had enough leg room and could see the road and lean back at the same time. He was amazed at how the soft white leather hugged his frame. The car still had the faint new car smell, but the vanilla air freshener was doing its job. The dash board looked like the cockpit of a seven-forty-seven airplane. So many knobs and dials and buttons for different functions. For the life of him he couldn't find where the CD's would go and then when she tapped her cell phone and classical music began to play he remembered reading how cell phones were now mini computers and everything was digital. Soft classical music filled the space. It used to be his music of choice while reading or doing some soul searching on sleepless nights.

On his left, Jasmine was quiet with a soft smile on her face. She seemed at peace. She would glance over at him every so often, then focus back on the road.

Mag was relaxed and his mind drifted back to his plan. He would start off by getting dropped off at a decent hotel and would then pick out a good travel guide and go from there. He remembered you had to make the plan then work the plan. Nothing would go as planned.

Now that his thirty eight year old body was relaxed and settled, he looked out at the country side and thought about what he knew about the city of San Antonio. He figured it wasn't a bad place to start off at after all.

If he remembered correctly from his studies, at one time no one really knew who the hell owned the land of San Antonio. Spain had claimed it, then France, then suspiciously the U.S., thought that Thomas Jefferson had really bought Texas from Napoleon in 1803 as part of the Louisiana purchase; And last but not at all least, Mexico, just out from under the mighty hand of Spain had claimed it.

Mag remembered reading that in 1821 a man named Steven F. Austin, with a paper signed by authorities in Mexico, led settlers into the new country. Within fifteen years the new settlers had managed to overtake the Apaches that had inhabited the land. The new settlers grew fast in number, up to thirty thousand in just fifteen years in the city of Baxar alone, known as San Antonio de Baxar, or just plain San Antonio.

Everything changed real fast after that. Mexico saw the true potential in the land and saw that the settlers were growing too strong and felt they had to remind them who the land really belonged to. Mag remembered laughing when he first read the fact. It would be like letting a friend drive an old used car that you weren't using, he fixes it up and has it fitted with a custom paint job, has the interior redone, and puts some brand new rims on it; then out of nowhere you show up fifteen years down the road and remind him who's car he's really driving. Crazy how something can be right and wrong at the same time.

The Mexicans wanted to send a clear message that Texas was their land and so a power struggle was born that lead to what's known today as the 'Battle at the Alamo'.

Mag glanced to his left. Jasmine still had a smile on her face, like she didn't have a care in the world. They made brief eye contact and then went back into their own thought worlds.

Mag smiled. He always smiled when he thought of the 182 soldiers that took on six thousand Mexican troops for thirteen days at the Alamo. He admired great men like William B. Travis, the co-commander and chief at the Alamo who some say was the first to die on March 6th, 1836 from a clean gunshot wound through the head.

He admired brave men like Davy Crockett and his Tennessee boys. Mag remembered reading that Crockett was known for playing his fiddle and singing songs. He was a master sharp shooter. In one season he was known to have killed one hundred and six bears with a rifle he called 'Old Betsy'. Crockett was found dead at the Alamo with twenty four of the dead enemy around him. In the hood today they would say: He went out like a soldier.

Mag's favorite was his boy James Bowie. As he leaned back in the car seat he remembered how Bowie was born in a place called Logan county Kentucky in 1796. He was a young dare devil known for riding wild mustangs and the backs of alligators. At 6'1" and 180 pounds, Bowie was a complex man that knew how to do two things good that Mag admired: fight and make money.

Mag loved the story of how Bowie killed a man named Major Wright and his friend Alfred Blanchard within seconds of one another only using a knife. The crazy thing was he had just been shot right before he killed them. He was known as a man who never lost a fight but had never started one either. Bowie's knife became legendary.

Mag also admired Bowie's hustle game of getting that money. At one time Bowie had listed his assets at a quarter of a million dollars. Tragedy struck Bowie in 1833. He lost his wife and kids to a cholera outbreak. Some say that this event killed his soul. Mag didn't have kids yet but he knew the pain of losing someone close to you. His dad had shot and killed his mother when he was just a teenager. Five years later he was in prison at the early age of nineteen.

A man named John T. Mason was a land shark whose New York company owned six million five hundred acres of Texas land and guess who his deputy administrator was: James Bowie.

Mag used common sense and figured that his boy Bowie had joined the Texas army to fight for the land that he was in charge of protecting. Rumor has it that Bowie died three deaths. The first in 1833 when he lost his wife and kids, the second when he fell from a scaffold from atop the Alamo which left him semi-conscious and bed ridden, and his last stand was in the Alamo chapel. The Mexicans burst through the door and froze when they thought they saw a ghost, which was really Bowie's pale skin. Bowie began firing and took many with him in the end. He too went out like a soldier and Mag respected that about him.

The Mexicans started blowing the victory horn over and over and over again. Mag woke up not knowing that he had drifted. The horn was not the Mexicans. It was an angry driver behind them mad that he'd been cut off.

"What the hell is. . . ?" Mag twisted in his seat to get a better look at the old man shaking his fist towards them. Spit was flying out of his mouth and fury was in his eyes. The car windows muffled his words.

Jasmine had a playful grin on her face as the old man pulled off in search of another parking spot. "He was a little slow for the beamer," she said. "Old people shouldn't be driving anyway."

Mag said, "You keep playing with them old people you want to, they're already at the end of they're life. What they got to lose? And you know damn well Texas got that new open carry law. Road rage at all time highs, you trippin!"

She seemed to ignore Mag's comments in a playful manner. She was biting at the end of one of her thumb nails. Her body was twisted halfway in her seat facing Mag's direction. Her dreamy bedroom eyes giving a clear message: 'I want you bad, Mag.' He broke her eye contact, not wanting to get caught in the web of her gaze and because all of a sudden his conscious mind finally caught up to the fact that they were parked. They were parked in between a CTS Cadillac and a huge Dodge Ram truck.

Mag said, "Where we at?"

He noticed that she took a deep breath before she started to speak. "Listen, I had this whole day planned out for my Uncle Torrez as a coming home surprise." She was speaking fast. "A shopping spree here at River Center Mall allowing him to get all the things that he needed. After this I have more surprises for him back at my home. I have a Jacuzzi tub I was going to allow him to enjoy before later taking him to one of San Antonio's historical restaurants."

The car was in park but it was still running. Soft air was coming out of the vents, no music. She spoke a lot with her hands. Her brows were furrowed, almost like they were pleading. There was something deeply hidden behind them, maybe fear of failure or rejections. Mag couldn't put his finger on it. He'd have to keep watching for clues.

She continued, "I don't want to waste this day or allow my setback to have victory over my perspective. I just want to live in the moment and follow what God has purposed and it seems like you are definitely a part of that purpose. I can see that you have an independent spirit but allow me to help you for helping me, let me give the day to you that I had planned for my uncle, and after the restaurant tonight you're free to go."

Her last few words 'free to go' made the air in Mag's lungs feel a little lighter. He thought he was free.

Mag tugged at his collar unconsciously, "Look Jasmine, no man just out of prison like myself in his right mind would turn down a shopping spree and surprises. We had this conversation before I even got in the car with you and I told you about my dream and how important it was. I have to do this on my own, just me and my freedom, me and the open air, me choosing to engage when I want with people how I want. It's nothing personal against you beautiful. I just gotta do me!"

The sharp screech made Mag jump back. It was followed by Jasmine slamming her back hard against her seat, her knuckles were white from her squeezing the steering wheel.

Her voice cracked as she spoke in tears, "I just want to do something nice for you Mag! Why are you making this so hard? I poured my heart out to you about how I'm trying to keep a positive perspective like you encouraged me to do and you still don't understand." Her eyes were fire red. She slammed her head hard against the steering wheel and was about to do it again but Mag grabbed her shoulder.

Her expression was changing from hurt to anger. Mag caught himself feeling selfish only thinking about himself. Maybe he wasn't paying attention to what God was doing. Why was he so stuck on one thing anyway, especially when it was hurting someone else? His mind was thinking these things, but his spirit was singing a different tune. The red flags were evident. The temper tantrums any time she felt rejected showed a codependent personality. Mag could tell that acceptance from others was connected to her self esteem and overall self concept. Her hidden fury was like a raging volcano that could blow at any time. He didn't want to get burned by the lava when it did. He gave in to his logic: 'Maybe I've read too many damn psychology books and I'm overanalyzing her. Just go with the flow Mag and after you eat later start your personal journey of freedom. Right now live in the moment and share it with this beautiful woman.'

Mag rubbed her shoulder and said, "Alright, alright, listen. I'm being a little too inflexible and I need to lighten up a bit and have some fun. Please forgive me." Mag stuck his bottom lip out.

She looked over at Mag and rolled her teary eyes, her shoulders stopped heaving, her cry settled to a sniffle. She reached over and put her small hand on top of his and said, "You get on my nerves Mag, but I forgive you. Forgive me for acting this way.

I've been highly stressed since my husband disappeared a year ago. It's hard being so alone."

Another red flag flashed through Mag's mind, but he shook it off and felt bad about the way he had been so narrow minded. He promised himself that he would relax and enjoy her company for the rest of the day.

Mag reached over and wiped the tears from her eyes and then kissed his fingers. She slapped his hand lightly, "Gross."

"Anything to get that beautiful smile back," Mag said. "Let's get out of this car, shall we? My stomach sounds like an angry pit bull; and by the way, lets hurry inside cause I read somewhere that 80% of mall crime happens in the parking lot while 80% of security is inside." She looked around as she pushed the button on the keychain that locked the doors. She said, "Let's hope that old man don't know that fact about security!" They both playfully took off running towards the mall entrance.

CHAPTER 5: THE MALL

The air-conditioning inside the mall felt good in Mag's lungs and on his skin. He felt like a kid in a candy store. The air smelled of soap and perfumes. People of all kinds, shapes, and sizes passed them as they walked by the many merchants lined down the middle walkway. Mag's senses were all pulling him in different directions at the same time.

A little boy with auburn hair about five years old caught Mag's attention in a toy store trying out a potential remote control car. The scene made Mag smile. Maybe one day in the future he'd have a son, a wife, and a house. He smiled when he thought about a quote by Isak Dinesen, "God made the world round so we could never see too far down the road".

The old and the young couples holding hands and smiling made Mag wonder what being "in love" felt like. Mag was intrigued at how each soul was in its own world, only fully knowing its own journey, its own hardships, but at the same time how we all are so interconnected.

Jasmine's arm was hooked into his as they strolled through the mall. He didn't mind. He'd decided to be nice. She was already under a lot of stress and beside the point; she was drop dead gorgeous and fine. She was draggin-that-wagon too. He knew a blessing when he had one. The woman was classy and on top of that she seemed to have money to blow; at the same time Mag remembered something he learned a long time ago while in prison: everything that glitters ain't gold, and all money ain't good money.

Mag started to smell various types of food as they entered an area labeled 'food court'. On cue his stomach reminded him that it too was also now free and wanted to indulge in the various fruits of freedom immediately. Mag noticed a pizza place, a Micky D's, a place called Panda Express, and a Taco Bell.

"That's what I'm talking about, right there Jasmine." Mag was pointing in towards the Taco Bell. "That Taco Bell right there, I've been dreaming for years of sinking my teeth into the shell of a Doritos Taco."

Mag was beaming and that caused Jasmine to smile as they walked towards the establishment. Mag could tell that she was in a better mood. Her eyes were a little puffy but other than that you couldn't tell that she had been crying at all; now that Mag had relaxed she had peace.

They were fifth in line behind a girl dressed like a punk rocker. Mag guessed she was about seventeen. She had long dark hair, a leather vest with spikes everywhere, and dark jeans with a skull and crossbones chain hanging from her belt loop. Mag figured she had the munchies. She smelled like a pound.

Mag looked over his left shoulder and noticed a Wells Fargo bank about twenty yards away. He remembered the checks in his pocket, one for $100 from TDCJ and the other from his books for $12,800.

Mag said, "Hold our spot for me while I run over and check out this bank real quick, okay?"

"Do you need me to go with you?" She asked with concern. Mag gave her a look that said, "Really?"

She said, "Ok, ok, go and hurry back."

Mag trotted over to the bank surprised that the mall had so many establishments in one spot. He was greeted at the counter with a professional hand shake from a guy maybe in his early thirties, slightly going bald at the top.

"How can I help you sir? How may I assist you?"

Mag pulled the checks from his pocket and laid them on the counter. "I would like to put these funds into an account that would allow me to be able to withdraw them with a card when needed. Do you have that option available here?"

The process took about ten minutes and Mag had what the man said was a debit card with a total of $12,900 on it. Mag thanked the man for his service and walked off.

A young and attractive white girl winked her eye at Mag as he made his way back to the food court. He wanted to flirt back but he felt eyes watching from across the room. Knowing Jasmine had emotional issues, he didn't want to take the chance of upsetting her and causing an embarrassing scene. So much for being free.

Jasmine was already taking a seat in the courtyard with their tray of food and drinks when he made it back. He sat across from her rubbing his hands together anxiously ready to dig in. She'd gotten him three Doritos tacos and a grilled stuffed burrito.

"Did you miss me?" Mag asked.

"Oh, so much papi. Every second you were away my heart was aching and longing for your long awaited return." She rolled her eyes. Mag smiled.

The first bit of the taco exploded with flavor. He closed his eyes and enjoyed the moment. He noticed she only had a drink.

"You're not going to eat anything?"

"I get my fill by watching you," she said as she went down on the straw then back up again a couple of times. Under the table her foot was making its way up his leg. Her eyes locked on his.

Mag said, "Don't blame me if the python locks onto your foot and cuts off your circulation. My last name isn't Magnum for nothing."

She squealed and pulled her leg back in a playful manner, smiling, lust in her eyes. He finished up and then they finished shopping. She had to carry some of his bags. She'd spent over a thousand on him for new clothes and shoes, at every turn batting down his objections like a professional lawyer. Mag had boxers, undershirts, the works. She even bought him a leather billfold to store his ID and spare cash in. He never once slid his debit card while in the mall, not once.

By the time they got back to the car, the warm San Antonio sun was high in the sky. It was 2:00 pm and they were due at the restaurant at 7:00 pm. That meant they had five hours to kill.

Mag was anxious to see the Jacuzzi tub she'd mentioned earlier. He wanted to soak for a hours to wash away the nineteen years of prison filth from his pours. To actually soak in warm water, allowing your muscles and body to fully relax as you close your eyes, Mag couldn't wait. He could actually stay in the water as long as he wanted, no one yelling "one minute", cutting the water off while he had a body full of soap, or having to worry about the water going cold in mid December, or not really knowing who was waiting to get a sneak peak as soon as he took his boxers off.

Mag was even considering letting the python out to play. He knew he couldn't make that decision without deep thought. If the person handling the python wasn't ready mentally or physically, people could end up hurt or even dead.

CHAPTER 6: STACY

The cool June air felt good against Mag's skin coming through the sunroof and windows. He felt like a kid allowing his right hand to swim through the air currents, first allowing the air to flow over his enclosed fingers, then cupping his hand grabbing a fist full of the invisible air, loving it's resistance of anything trying to control it.

'Air,' he thought, 'I want to feel free like air.' In prison he saw thousands of men who were like automated robots following the routine of the system. At times he felt the same way. Now he almost felt like he was living under the Jasmine system of what to do and where to go.

'Four to five more hours of catering to her feelings, then I can finally exhale,' Mag thought, then smiled.

"This is my neighborhood," Jasmine said as she made the left turn. Mag couldn't believe some of the houses he was seeing. They were huge, right out of the Home Magazines he had flipped through in prison.

"Damn mami, you got it like this?" Mag asked.

"My husband owned a very lucrative consulting business. He was the highest paid consulting engineer in town. I don't want for anything, but you," she said as she winked her eye.

She made a right onto the main intersection, drove for about a block before she made the right into a Shell gas station. She parked in front of an empty gas pump on Mag's side of the car. They were parked behind an all white new model Jag. Mag guessed it was the F-type he'd seen advertised on TV.

"You go in and pay, and I'll pump the gas," she said as she handed him one hundred and fifty dollars, "and you can 'pump' later."

Mag shook his head and smiled. "I'm starting to see you're a freak and by the way, damn, how much is gas, ten dollars an gallon?"

"No silly, it's around three. Just pay for the fill up and use the rest to buy yourself snacks or maybe you may need some condoms for later, who knows?" She said with a smile.

Mag couldn't deny she had a sexy ass accent, and those bedroom eyes were addictive. Mag stepped out of the beamer feeling fresh. He'd given the New Balance shoes and outfit to a bum on the outside of the mall. He had changed into a pair of all black patent-leather J's, crispy white blue jeans with the hard crease, and a Jordan polo shirt that hugged his frame like a tailor made suit. His haircut was still fresh from the comb and razor cut he'd got from his Mexican homeboy Lopez a few days ago, a tight bald fade with the waves hitting up top. Yeah, he felt fresh, and the Curve cologne didn't hurt either.

Jasmine was already pumping the gas as he strolled passed the Jag towards the entrance. A bell dinged overhead as he opened the door. He was immediately met by cool air on the inside and the clean smell of the place. A woman who looked like she was carrying an uncomfortable extra thirty pounds gave him a nod with a look that said, 'what are you doing in these parts,' a statement, not a question. He just smiled at her and walked up to the counter.

I'm paying on pump six," Mag said. The lady whose nametag said she was Sue looked out at pump six at the BMW, then back at Mag with a look that said, 'damn drug dealers!' Mag smiled again when he thought about a quote by Rita Mae Brown that had stuck with him: About all you can do in life is be who you are. Some people will love you for you, most will love you for what you can do for them, and some won't like you at all.

Sue said, "She's still pumping. Get the things you need then come back. She should be finished by then and I can ring up your total."

Mag noticed that the lady had one hand on the counter and the other underneath. In the back he could hear the Slurpee machines whirling away. Mag gave Sue a superficial smile and walked towards the back left hand corner of the store.

Just being in the gas station felt liberating, so many options, so many choices, like commissary on steroids. He went to the last row, turned right, and was floored. The girl could have been Vanessa Williams at 22; 5'9", honey yellow skin, a posture that radiated confidence without even trying. Her hair was pulled back into a ponytail that sat on the back of her neck. Her body was stunning, flawless legs that looked like they tasted like the candy Werther's Originals dipped in honey. She was dressed casual in black heels, jean shorts that hugged her hips just right, and a white t-shirt that said SPURS on the back in black and grey letters.

Mag had to force himself to close his mouth. His heart rate had picked up a bit and butterflies stormed his stomach. He checked his breath, good, put his best stroll on and headed over to the area where she stood. He stood in line behind her and thought of something clever to say.

Mag said, "Excuse me," she stopped filling her cup halfway and turned around. It was as if he was looking into the Milky Way Galaxy. Her eyes were green with twists and turns of hazel. They both held eye to eye contact and smiled.

Mag continued, "I was about to say something about you looking like an expert slurpee maker on what flavors go good together or something to that effect, but umm," they both laughed nervously, "to be honest I want to tell you that you are amazingly beautiful, and now that I've been blessed to look into your eyes I can see that you have an intelligent spirit that I assume a lot of people neglect to see because of their focus on your beauty."

Mag held his breath for her response.

She said, "Wow, thank you. That was better than the slurpee thing. I'm so tired of lame lines, and since we're being so honest, I, um, saw you walking towards the store and I had to run back to this corner to compose myself. I really didn't even plan on getting a slurpee."

They both burst out laughing. The laughter made Mag relax. It had been ages since he had been in the presence of a woman whom made him feel this way.

"My name is Ty Magnum, but you can call me Mag. What's yours?"

"Stacy Jones, and it's very nice to meet a man who isn't afraid to just say hi and speak it like you feel it. For some reason men are intimidated by self confident women with strong minds."

"Well at this moment I'm thankful for those types of men because it's because of them that you're not taken. Being in your presence makes me feel like a star, Stacy. How about we finish this conversation tomorrow night, my treat?"

She smiled, "Oh, and he's fast on his feet too I see. Yes, Mr. Mag, tomorrow night would be perfect since I don't have practice." She handed Mag a card with her name and number on it and said, "Call me around three. I know the perfect place to go."

She began to walk off, "Stacy," she stopped four feet away and turned around, "you mentioned practice. What do you play?" Mag asked.

"I'm a San Antonio Spurs cheerleader and I don't play. Make sure you call me, Mag." She turned, paid at the counter for gas and the half filled slurpee, and headed towards the white Jag. As she pulled out she waved at Mag inside the store and was gone.

Mag was on cloud nine as he filled the two slurpees, picked up a pack of winter fresh gum, and headed for the counter. He noticed the cashiers hand slide back beneath the counter. His total was seventy four fifty. He pocketed the change and told the heavyset lady, "Sorry for your wait," making sure to put emphasis on the word 'weight'.

Mag pushed open the door with his back and headed towards the beamer. The sun, traffic, and energy of just being free made him smile again. He silently thanked God for his grace. Jasmine was sitting in the car glaring at him through the windshield. She leaned over her seat and pushed open the door for him to get in. He placed the slurpees in the cup holder and shut the door.

"I hope you like blue mango, and by the way you gave me like seventy dollars too much for snacks." Mag tried to hand her the money.

She was gripping the steering wheel looking straight ahead. She was clearly shaken, her face flushed red, laser focus ahead. She drew in a long slow breath then let it out slow. She was focused on something on the outside of the windshield not inside her mind. She breathed in slow and then out slower. Mag slowed his words.

"Are you ok Jasmine? Do I need to do something? What's wrong?"

She shook her head quick in a snapping motion, looked in his direction and smiled. She let out another deep breath.

She said, "That girl, she waved, and I thought . . . you know what, it's nothing. I'm ok."

"You thought what, Jasmine?" Mag asked.

Her voice raised an octave, "I said its nothing! I'm ok. Ok?"

Mag had to take his own deep breath and straighten in his seat sipping on his blue mango slurpee. 'This woman is really emotionally damaged. This night can't end sooner.' Mag thought as she navigated the streets towards her house.

CHAPTER 7: THE CHEESE

Mag believed that everything happened for a reason on this journey we call life. He also believed that trials and tribulations were the key ingredient in growth mentally and spiritually. He understood that there was no education like adversity and that in any given situation there is no strength gained where there is no struggle. He was searching hard for the lesson he was destined to learn from getting in the car with this woman. At times he felt like W.B. Yeats when he said: 'If suffering brings wisdom, I would wish to be less wise.' What he knew for sure was the fact that anytime you bring something into your life, you invited the good and the bad, the yin and the yang. He had made his choice.

"We're here," Jasmine said with cheer in her voice.

Mag's thoughts dissolved and what filled his vision caused him to sit up in his seat. She pushed a number on the key pad and the solid iron black and gold gate opened for them. Jasmine smiled as she pulled into the long driveway and up to the house. It was massive. He wouldn't have been surprised to see Tony Parker or Big Tim Duncan picking up their newspaper next door.

"Damn baby! You stay in all this by yourself?" Mag asked.

"In the main house, yes. My dad stays in the house out back."

Mag couldn't believe his good fortune. He definitely now believed that God's hands were on him and this part of his journey. As they gathered his things from the car, Mag could do nothing but stare at the house.

The three story architecture design was modern and elegant, lots of windows adorned the house and the roof had oval shaped brick shingles. The big tree in the front of the property and those that seemed to hug the home made it seem as if it sat inside of an enchanted forest. As they neared the front door, Mag loved the two panthers that sat at each side of the grand porch. He could tell that the designs on the massive oak-wood door were inspired from ancient Rome. The door handle was shiny gold plated.

"This looks like some shit I used to see on MTV's Cribs. I must say, you are truly full of surprises," Mag said. She just chuckled.

Mag took his bags from her as she unlocked the door and couldn't help but see her pink thong playing peek-a-boo above her shorts. They stepped inside. The high ceiling caught Mag's attention first. Next, he couldn't help but notice the double stairs that gave you two ways to get to the next level. The openness was stunning.

"Wow," was all Mag could say. The contrast from his cell to this was mind blowing. Jasmine stood behind him to allow him to get an eye full.

"The living room and kitchen are the primary rooms on this floor." Far off to his right Mag could see part of the massive living room and to his left the opening leading into the kitchen.

She said, "Follow me and I'll show you where you'll be staying. I mean changing."

"I heard that. You want your boy to stay with you. I ain't gonna lie. This is almost hard to believe. Just hours ago I was in a cell where I could touch each side of the cell with outstretched arms.

Now look." Mag spread his arms and spun in a circle. Jasmine just smiled.

"You got to be . . ." was all Mag could get out as they stepped onto the second floor and she opened the theater room door. Plush seating filled the room and the high def TV had to be at least 90 inches. She touched a knob and the lighting lit up a little brighter so that Mag could get a better look.

"Anytime you want to chill and Netflix, I'm available. Maybe after dinner," she said with hope in her voice.

Mag walked around the room and felt on the couches. He fell back on the soft pillows and let them cushion his fall. As Mag got back up she said, "The two hallways that you saw when we first got to this floor hold the guest rooms and on the very top floor are the two master bedrooms. One is mine and the other was my late husbands. You'll bathe and get ready in his old room, and yes it's been cleaned."

Mag followed her up a second set of stairs that spiraled up to the third floor. Her room was to the left and his was to the right she explained. He turned towards the room she said was his for the evening.

She said, "Come and take a peek at my room before you go and get ready. I want to show you something."

"You not crazy like that lady in that movie Misery are you?" Mag asked.

"Of course not, silly," she said in the accent and playfully hit Mag in his chest, "unless of course you 'drive me crazy'."

Mag smiled and laid his bags by his door and followed her. She opened her door and said, "ta-da," pointing at the huge California King. The bed was suspended in mid-air at least 10 feet, held in place by four velvet ropes at each corner of her bed and somehow mounted to a round plate in her ceiling.

The room was spacious and smelled of perfume.

"How the hell do you get into that thing?" Mag asked, curious.

She pushed a button on a remote and the bed began to descend, stopping two feet from the ground.

"Wow, impressive," he said.

Jasmine pushed another button and the bed started to go back up but was spinning in slow circles. The room darkened and different color lights flashed from bulbs in the ceiling. Mag felt a hand on his shoulder, caressing the muscles there. Then two hands. For the moment, Mag closed his eyes as her hands eased years of tension from his shoulders. It had been so long since a woman had touched him the way she was. Before he knew it, his manhood was at full attention, his mind a thousand miles away, lost in comfort-land. Her hands headed south, caressing all the way down. Her hands slipped past the V shape of his waist-line into his boxers; she took hold of the python. She sucked in a quick breath of amazement. It broke the trance.

"Oh, whoa, woah, woah, mami," Mag said as he recomposed himself and stepped away towards the door. She licked her lips. Mag heard the click of a button and the lights came on and the bed stopped spinning. Mag could now clearly see the lust in her eyes. She licked her lips again and looked down as if saying she wanted to taste him.

"No wonder you keep him caged up," she said.

"I got to mami. The wrong person handle him the wrong way and they could get bit and we don't want that." Mag walked out of the room.

"I left you a surprise on the middle of the bed, well, I mean, it was for my uncle but it's yours now. I hope you like it. Be ready to go in a couple of hours."

"I got you mami. I'll meet you downstairs." He entered the room.

The bed was built into the wall. A massive lion's head was the headboard and you had to walk into his mouth in order to lay on his tongue. His tongue had to be bigger than a California

King mattress. Mag pulled a string hanging from the roof of his mouth and red light lit up the space. Mag couldn't believe the design, what money could buy if only you had the imagination.

To the left of the lion's head stood a night stand made of solid oak and trimmed in gold. The far left side of the room contained a door that lead to a walk-in closet. To the far right of the room was the master bath. Mag walked to the master bath and flipped on the light and was astonished. The Jacuzzi tub was right out of the movies. If Scarface would have been sitting in it he wouldn't have been surprised. It was built into the floor and trimmed in gold. A flat screen TV at least seventy five inches hung on the wall in front of the Jacuzzi.

Mag dropped his bags outside the door and walked into the restroom/spa. To the far left of the room stood a shower encased in see-through glass. Mag had taken countless showers in prison and had no intention of taking one at the moment.

Mag plugged the Jacuzzi and began to fill it with body soothing warm water. He found a bubble solution on the sink and applied it to the water. It immediately started to sud up. Mag smiled. He figured it would take at least five to ten minutes to fill the massive Jacuzzi and so he returned to the bedroom. Mag hit the switch for the ceiling fan. The room was clean but smelled kind of stale from the lack of use.

Mag noticed a package in the center of the bed and remembered what Jasmine had said about his surprise in the middle of the bed. Mag slipped out of his shirt and shoes, and hopped onto the plush lion's tongue. He grabbed the package and then positioned his back against the huge pillows. Mag had his legs fully outstretched and he was smiling. He had the urge to get up and jump up and down on the bed but the package had his attention and he didn't know if the room had cameras.

The outside of the package said Kay Jewelers in fancy gold lettering. Mag remembered hearing the trademark jingle on TV: every kiss begins with Kay. The package contained two boxes. One was about four inches long and the other a ring box. Mag pulled the ring box out first and opened it. He was speechless.

The huge pinky ring was in the shape of a lion's head with a full golden mane. His eyes were yellow diamonds and in his mouth he held a massive, fine-cut, one karat diamond. He didn't notice that his mouth was open. Mag tried the ring on. It fit perfect. He figured he and Torrez must have had the same size finger. He extended his left arm to get a better view, beautiful.

He couldn't believe it. If he were to write his boy Buddy and tell him his story thus far it would be hard for him to believe; that made him think he had to buy a camera ASAP. Pictures in prison were almost more valuable than commissary. He agreed with Susan Sontag when she said: 'Today everything exists to end in a photograph.' Moments like this were fleeting.

Mag pulled the other box from the packaging and shook it to see if he could guess what it was. Whatever it was, it was heavy and solid. Both good things when it came to jewelry. Mag opened the box and shot up in the bed like a rocket. He couldn't believe his eyes. "Are you shitting me?!" He said it to the watch as if it could speak back. Now he was jumping. The Rolex was a beautiful piece. Solid crushed diamonds made up the wrist band. The face was trimmed in gold. Mag watched the second hand close to see if it glided or ticked. It glided. He smiled. It was a real Rolex. He put it on the same hand as his new ring and together they looked like the moon and the stars. He bounced on the bed some more.

He had been out of prison for ten hours and he had a ten thousand dollar watch on his wrist and there was no telling how much the ring cost. He was ecstatic. Maybe God was blessing him for the nineteen years of hardship he had just endured; on his deathbed Samuel Butler said: 'I have written that life is ninety-nine percent chance. I wish to correct this figure to one hundred percent.' Maybe it was chance. Whatever it was, he was now thankful that he had gotten in that car with Jasmine.

A quick flash of thought shot through his mind: 'How much cheese does a mouse get to eat before the trap snaps on him?'

Mag shook the thought off and looked at the Rolex and the ring on his left arm. He remembered the running water and ran into the bathroom and turned it off. It was about five inches from the top, perfect. Back in the room, Mag removed the Rolex and the ring and placed them on the dresser. He looked down at his bags and was considering what to wear. He smiled. What a beautiful dilemma to have. He figured she might have some fancy place in mind so he decided to dress up just in case.

She's bought him six pairs of shoes; three pairs of Jordans and three pairs of dress shoes. He chose the all white gators with the 14k buckle. From his clothes he chose to wear his all black pre-pressed Gucci slacks. For his shirt he chose a shirt made of smooth silky feeling material. It was a button up, white with a gold lion's head on the back. White on white, shoes and shirt both sprinkled with gold. He loved it. 'Perfect place at the perfect time,' he thought, 'perfect place at the perfect time.'

CHAPTER 8: LORA

Mag stripped down to his boxers and did a quick work-out. He did twenty sets of fifty push-ups. The work-out took him twenty minutes. He walked back into the bathroom and stopped to admire the hard work he had put into his body, thankful that he hadn't allowed himself to lay around prison and get fat and lazy like a lot of guys he knew. He used a quote from Muhammad Ali as motivation: 'I hate every minute of training, but I said, "suffer now and live the rest of your life as a champion".' Mag suffered on that hot rec yard for years and he was now reaping the benefits of his hard work. He came up with a program that he called the MBS system of excellence. In this program the M stood for mind, the B stood for body, and the S stood for spirit. If each day he planted a seed of growth in each of these areas, he knew he was doing his time and not just passing it like he saw a lot of men doing in front of the TV all day long or playing board games.

Mag dipped his foot into the water. It had cooled but not by much. He slipped off his boxers and slid into the warm bubbly water. The water hugged his entire body and immediately started to sooth his muscles. He noticed a square box laying on a make-shift stand near the tub and grabbed it. It was a touch screen device with what looked like a waterproof cover around it. It came to life when Mag tapped the user interface screen. One icon was labeled 'Jacuzzi' and the other 'lights'. He chose the 'Jacuzzi' option and when he pushed the button the water around him immediately began to move. He pressed the option that said 'massage' and water pressure began to move in circles all over his back, underneath his legs, and his feet. He leaned back in the tub and smiled. He noticed an option to make the water warmer and he raised the temp a few degrees. He was in heaven.

He touched the screen tab that opened the 'light' options and dimmed them a bit. Automatically a picture image of a fireplace appeared on the flat screen. "All I need now is a Cuban cigar and a glass of wine and Scarface couldn't tell me nothing."

Mag set the iPad remote down and relaxed his body, allowing his mind to drift off to never never land for a moment. For a moment he took his mind off of everything. For nineteen years he'd walked around on alert, focused and ready. Even in his sleep he'd trained himself to be semi-conscious of danger. A sewing needle dropping to the ground could wake him. You had to be like that in prison. One moment you could be asleep and the next your cell door could roll open and five massive barbarians could be rushing in planning on changing your name from Magnum to Maggy.

But in this moment he allowed himself to truly relax as he let the force of the water massage away nineteen years of built up tension. He served his time like a man, paid for the things he had to pay off in the spiritual world traf justice, and he deserved to feel the peace that he felt in this moment. When men in prison use to complain to Mag about the amount of time they were doing, Mag would try to explain to them the principle of justice but to no avail; the victimizer was now in his mind a victim but

Mag knew that justice is: 'word for word, action for action, and thought for thought. What comes back to the initiator is not just what they've done, but also everything that grows out of what they've done.' Mag had learned this wisdom from the great W. James Dennis.

'How much cheese does a mouse get to eat before the trap snaps him?' There was that voice again. What did it mean? His subconscious was trying to tell him something but he couldn't put his finger on it and he wanted to relax not focus on serious shit at the moment. Life was good. He was blessed. He shook it off and thought about his plan: enjoy the night, find out a way to plant seeds of encouragement into Jasmine's soul, and maybe even come back and let the python play. Mag couldn't exactly put his finger on Jasmine's condition, but she definitely was co-dependent and had an aggressive fear of abandonment. Mag wondered what her story was. During dinner he would have to listen intently and ask the right questions, he knew that 85% of all good questions came through listening skills. He had to at least try to help this woman. It was the least he could do for all that she had given him.

Mag planned to leave early that morning to get a room. Then he would call Stacy in hopes of spending a little time before he saw the rest of the city or moved on.

Mag found a wash rag and soap and used it to scrub the rest of prison from his skin. He exited the tub twenty minutes later, feeling good about his plan. Nothing would go as planned!

He wrapped himself in a towel and entered his room. He heard a light tap at the door.

"Yeah, you miss me already?" Mag asked.

"Yes, of course, but I need some advice on what dress to wear tonight. What's your fashion game like? Can you help?" She asked.

"Yeah, come in," Mag said.

Jasmine came in the room holding two dresses. The light coming through the door illuminated her already see-through night gown. Mag could see everything and her body was flawless. She knew exactly what she was doing.

Underneath the towel Mag was already rising. The smoothness of her skin, the coke-bottle shape, the perfect symmetry of her breasts, the flow of her areolas into her nipples, and the hairless mound of flesh between her legs was almost too much for Mag to handle. He knew in his heart that he would only complicate things if he took things to a physical level at this point. That reasoning was the only thing stopping him. He willed himself to look at the dresses. She was smiling, looking at the bulge in his towel. She knew the exact effect she was having on him.

"The white one with the gold belt," Mag said, "it goes with that outfit you got me out of Dillard's. I'm wearing it tonight." His eyes kept going from the dresses to her nipples.

"Thank you," she said as she turned to leave, making sure to sway that ass back and forth for emphasis. Right before she entered her room she looked back at Mag and winked.

"I'll meet you downstairs in thirty, ok?" she said.

Mag nodded, closed his door and dressed thinking, 'a better question would be how long does the mouse look at the cheese before he decides to taste it?'

Jasmine was already downstairs waiting at the door for him as he came off of the bottom step.

"I see you found your gift," she said.

Mag looked down at his left wrist and pinky finger and smiled.

"Thank you really doesn't express my gratitude. I might have to find a better way later to express myself," Mag said playfully.

"It really looks good on you Mag, really. I'm glad you like it."

"You look stunning yourself mami. Together we killin the game. Come here and let me feel how you feel in my arms again."

She walked over and Mag held her, letting his hands slip down over her bump and inhale her perfume. He took her right hand and spun her around. The elegant backless dress hugged her frame with precision. Her gold heels matched her belt and her earrings. Her hair was curled into massive Shirley Temple curls that fell over each side of her shoulders. The light touch of make-up on her face complimented her high cheekbones perfectly. Mag released her and they locked eyes. A quick shot of sadness struck Mag's soul. 'How could such a beautiful woman be so damaged internally?' He had to find out why.

"You ready, beautiful?" Mag asked.

"After you," she said as she opened the door.

It took them only fifteen minutes to get to their destination. It was 6:45 and the sun was just deciding to take a nap.

They turned onto a street called Commerce and parked. The air outside the car was cool and refreshing.

"A friend of mine told me this place was delicious," Jasmine said as they walked towards the door.

The name above the door said the place was called Delicatessen. Mag couldn't begin to pronounce the name. The inside of the restaurant had a historical feel. The vintage tile floor, pressed tin ceiling, and wood and limestone interior gave the place an old world atmosphere. Mag felt they were overdressed.

They were seated in one of the three oak booths nearest the street.

"What would you like to drink while you look over the menu?" The waitress asked.

She was beautiful. Long auburn hair, aqua blue eyes, leggy, her smile was like a magnet. A natural all American beauty.

"What would you suggest we drink, Lora?" Mag asked.

She looked down at her name tag, "Oh, I'm sorry. I didn't introduce myself. I'm Lora, as you've already read."

She extended her hand and both Mag and Jasmine shook it.

She said, "I'm really not supposed to be shaking hands because of our Covid-19 policy, but ya'll look famous and I couldn't help myself."

"No, we're not famous, and plus I got both my shots and the booster. You good ma," Mag said.

"I'm fully vaccinated too," Jasmine added, "Thank you for the compliment."

"We are only allowing 50% capacity right now so ya'll should have a smooth, uncrowded affair." Lora said.

The eye contact lingered between Mag and Lora on the word 'affair'.

Lora said, "Our restaurant is one of the oldest eateries in town with almost 100 years of service. I would suggest ya'll try our famous root-beer."

"What makes it so famous?" Jasmine asked sounding a little annoyed.

"Well, when prohibition hit San Antonio, the Germans could no longer enjoy their schooners of beer, so the owner, Papa Fritz, developed a supercharged recipe for root-beer."

"What's in it?" Mag asked curious.

"Our root-beer is made by Son Beverages of San Antonio using the same formula, but we add egg whites to give it that special Papa Fritz flavor."

Mag was looking deep into Lora's eyes as she talked, which caused her to blush and smile. Jasmine leaned back in her chair and crossed her arms.

Mag said, "The root-beer sounds great. I'll have one. How about you, Jazzy?"

"I'll take whatever!" She said, feisty.

Lora eyed Mag, "Yeah, two root-beers will be fine, Lora. We'll be ready to order when you return." Mag said. Lora walked off.

"What's your issue all of a sudden?" Mag asked.

"What do you think?" Jasmine asked. "I see the way she's looking at you, and you looking right back!"

"Come on now mami, we came out here to have a good time. You act like I'm a three hundred pound ugly guy or something. Of course women are going to look at me, and I've got eyes too. Just relax. It's nothing major. If we were married or even together we both would be out of line, but Jazzy, we young and single. I'm enjoying myself. Chill."

"Well she don't know what we are and I don't like it. She needs to stop before I lose my patience. And you could at least respect me enough to give me this special night and then 'do you' when it's not in my face!"

Mag wasn't the one to go back and forth and so he just let it go. For some reason he had a strong feeling in his soul that he was being watched. He looked around the room and besides them there was only four other couples. No one was paying attention to them. Mag looked out the window nearest him and across the street he noticed a man dressed in all black that seemed to be staring right at him. He was leaning up against a pole looking right in his direction.

"So what are you going to eat, Mr. Good Looking?" Jasmine asked. Mag broke his focus from the man across the street and took a look at the menu.

He said, "I don't know what the hell bratwurst, wiener schnitzel, braunschweiger or any other German dish is. Do you?"

She laughed at the way he said the names. She shook her head no and kept looking at the menu. As Mag kept looking at the menu he started to see American dishes towards the bottom. He looked out the window. The man was gone.

Lora was back with their drinks. They were in big heavy glasses.

"Here you go," Lora said. "Have ya'll decided what you'll be eating tonight?" She asked with a German accent.

"Um, yeah, I think I'll have the Reuben sandwich," Mag said.

"And for you?" Lora asked in Jasmine's direction.

I'll have the Shilo's split pea soup."

"Both good choices," Lora said. "And by the way, I must say ya'll are a very beautiful couple."

"Thanks, but we're just friends out enjoying the night." Mag said.

If looks could kill Mag would be dead. It was written all over Jasmine's face.

"I know you have to beat your other friends off with a stick," Lora said in the direction of Jasmine.

Mag noticed Jasmine pick up the butter knife. She had it gripped tight right side up. She was glaring at Lora, her eyes and face flushed red.

The front door to the establishment opened and the man dressed in all black from across the street was coming right at Mag. He walked right up to their booth and took the knife right out of Jasmine's hand .The guy eyed Lora and she took off for the food. Jasmine stood and buried her head into the man's chest.

There was something familiar about the guy. Mag couldn't put his finger on it. The man had a hard-lined face from stress or maybe smoking. It was evident to Mag the man had lived a hard life. Why was he here? And why the hell was he watching Mag in all black from across the street?

He was 5'8", about 185, hard lean body. He had those short thick fingers, strong looking hands. He was at least fifty for sure, but his body could pass for a healthy forty.

He was looking at Mag hard as he held onto Jasmine. Mag could tell instantly that Jasmine felt safe in his arms, no doubt. His eyes were as dark as coal; and then it hit Mag, he had the same eyes as Torrez. They had to be either brothers or very close cousins. What the hell was going on? Mag held eye contact with the man making sure he knew that there was no punk in his blood.

Jasmine and the man finally broke their embrace. The man looked away from Mag and stroked Jasmine's hair in a comforting manner. For the third time that day she wiped tears from her eyes.

"Dad, this is Ty Magnum. Ty, this is my dad, Victor Cruz." She said.

Mag extended his hand. Victor ignored the gesture. Mag pulled his hand back.

"Baby, go use the restroom while papa speaks to this young man," Victor said.

"Daaaad," Jasmine said.

"What did I say," Victor said with an authoritative look and tone. Jasmine walked off towards the restroom eyeing Mag as if to say, 'it's going to be alright'.

Victor took Jasmine's seat and motioned for Mag to have a seat. Mag had subconsciously stood and hadn't even realized it. Mag took a deep breath and took a seat.

Victor said, "Listen to me and listen closely. My baby girl deserves the very best and that's what she's going to get. Her mom died when she was only thirteen. She's all I got left. Now I know all about you pretty boys with the eyes and all that shit thinking you can roll in and spit game and manipulate a come-up. If that's what you thinking you sadly mistaken! Watch how you handle her heart. She's been through a lot and I'm the one who put her through most of it. I'll be damned if I let someone else hurt her!" Victor slammed his fist on the table and walked off leaving Mag no chance to refute his comments. Mag heard a bell ding and looked in the direction of the front door. Victor stopped, turned, and said, "She's not like most women," and then he was gone.

Mag was a little disturbed but nothing too serious. 'What did he mean by she's not like other women,' Mag thought. Mag didn't fear any man but there was something about Victor's eyes that were unsettling. 'Watch how you handle her heart,' Mag repeated the words to himself.

"Where'd my dad go?" Jasmine asked breaking his thoughts. Lost in thought Mag hadn't even noticed her walk up. Mag took a sip of his root beer before he answered. It was full bodied and creamy with a strong root beer flavor, sweet but not overly.

"He left," Mag said. "He basically said to treat you right and that you've been through a lot in life."

"Yeah, my dad is a little overprotective, more so than most. He's sixty three years old but is still active and in shape for his age. He lives on three acres of land behind my house in a large wooden cabin."

She had Mag's full attention.

"Why do you feel that he is overprotective?" Mag asked.

"Well it's a mixture of things," she said, "but it's mostly because when he was young he was a runner for the Mexican mafia, a cartel family. His cargo was stolen by a rival gang and when he tried to explain it to his boss they didn't believe him. One night they gave him a mission that he knew would be his last and so he escaped."

Lora was back with the food. She put it down and left immediately.

Jasmine continued, "His cartel family found out where I went to school." She swallowed hard. Mag could tell going back to that terrible time was difficult. "They took me from school in Mexico, told me that my dad had had an accident and I needed to hurry to the hospital. They told my dad something different, that he had a week to get them their drugs back or twenty five thousand dollars or things would happen to me he didn't want to imagine."

Tears were forming in her eyes threatening to spill over. Mag was listening to her like a woman listening to her unborn baby's heartbeat for the first time. He was looking into her soul and he saw raw and unhealed pain.

She continued, "My dad came up with the money, my entire family came together, but by the time they came to get me the damage to my soul was already done. The things they did to me that week still haunt me until this day."

Mag reached across the table and wiped the freshly fallen tears from her face.

Mag asked, "Did you explain to your dad what happened to you?"

"At first I tried to spare him the details. He kept pressing me, and so I finally told him and he was never the same. Something in him broke and his eyes grew a shade darker. Those guys disappeared and we left Mexico never to return. He has watched over me closely since we left."

Mag felt it an odd time to take a bite of his food. He took a sip of root beer instead.

"Have you taken any steps to heal from your wounds?"

"You know, I just do my best to put it behind me. I don't think about it." She said.

Mag could sense a defensive tone. He also noticed that she'd picked up her fork as to say 'I'm really hungry'.

She said, "You know what, enough about me. Tell me about your childhood."

She took a bite of her pea soup, and gave an approving nod that meant it was good. Mag took that as a cue and began eating as he thought about how he was going to answer her question.

Mag started with a lie, "Well, my mother died when she was having me." The fact that his father had shot and killed his mother when he was a teen was not something that he shared openly.

He continued, "I was raised by my dad. He and my granddad taught me everything I know. We struggled in poverty and so my dad started selling drugs and the bodies of women as a means of survival. I have an older sister somewhere. My dad couldn't keep us both. She was raised by my dad's sister in Wichita Falls. Maybe she's still there. I don't know. I'll eventually make my way through there and find her one day."

"So where is your father now?" Jasmine asked.

Mag shrugged, took a sip of his root beer before answering, "He never wrote me one time in prison, sent money a few times. I don't know if he is still alive, in prison, or out there somewhere; I don't really think about it and really don't care."

They both went quiet for a while, allowing what they'd heard to soak in.

"Wow, it must feel lonely not to have family," Jasmine said.

It was Mag's turn to get defensive, "And I don't need one! I'm going to buy my dream car, an old school drop top Cadillac, and paint it Dallas Cowboy's two-toned gray and blue, and travel the entire state of Texas. Just me and the open road."

Through his peripheral vision Mag could see Lora approaching their table.

She said, "Is everything good? Can I get you anything?" She said it in her usual bubbly voice. Mag had to wonder if she knew that only fifteen minutes ago she could have been stabbed. Maybe she just wanted a good tip, or she was just blinded by the undercurrent attractive energy that she felt when she looked into Mag's eyes.

"Fun fact," Lora said, "the very booth that you guys are sitting in came from a late 1800's ice cream parlor and the antiques collector who sold them to this place said that before that they were in a class B bawdy house in San Antonio's red light district."

Mag looked down at the seat, "A bawdy house, I bet all kinds of things have went down right where we are sitting at."

Lora said, "Yeah, all kinds of good things," with a smile. She was looking directly into Mag's eyes as she responded.

The volcano erupted! Before Mag could react, the heavy root beer mug was up in the air and coming down hard towards Lora's head. The thud sound of thick solid glass connecting with skull was unmistakable.

It seemed to Mag as if the scene unfolding in front of him was moving in slow motion. When Lora hit the ground limp with a thud everything sped up.

Jasmine moved with demented speed and was upon Lora's unconscious body with the glass raised high, clinched tight in her hands. Mag grabbed her from behind and lifted her and walked towards the exit. The glass hit the ground. Jasmine's arms and legs were flailing everywhere. The other customers in the place had shocked looks on their faces as they gazed upon the large knot forming on the left side of Lora's head. Mag carried Jasmine all the way back to the car.

"Where are the fucking keys Jasmine." Mag asked in the form of a command, not a question.

"In my purse on the table," she was breathing hard, an evil look in her eyes.

Mag said, "Stay RIGHT here, you hear me!"

A weird satisfaction shown in Jasmine's eyes at the command. It was as if she got a thrill at being controlled.

Mag dashed across the street and back into the establishment. People were gathered around Lora pressing a towel with ice in it onto her head.

"Is she breathing?" Mag heard one say.

"Yes," another answered.

Mag looked towards their table and a white guy with a grey button up shirt had his hand inside of Jasmine's purse. Mag guessed he was looking for her ID.

"Hey!" Mag yelled towards the man, "Get your hand out of my wife shit!" The guy backed up.

Mag grabbed Jasmine's purse from the table, pulled out his wallet and left seventy dollars on the table. It most likely wouldn't cover her medical bills but it was something.

He noticed people on their phones, some talking to the police and others getting instructions from 911 operators. He knew he had to get moving fast. An ex-con, an assault with a makeshift weapon just didn't mix and come out a good result. He ran back to the BMW.

"Get in! I'm driving. Just give me directions on getting back to the house." Mag said.

Jasmine unfolded her arms in the passenger side and pressed a few buttons on the cockpit dash and a GPS system popped up.

"Just follow the arrow. It will lead you."

About half a block down the road a woman's voice said 'turn left' and the arrow made the left hand turn. Mag followed directions. He had slight nerves driving after nineteen years but his adrenaline was fueling him. He was hoping no one gave the police a description of the car because driving without a license could either get you a ticket or a night in jail.

As he drove towards the house he heard a voice say in his head, 'the cheese is your weakness.'

Chapter 9: Red Flag

It only took ten minutes to get back to the house. Mag's driving was rusty but it was like riding a bike, you never forgot how. As a young teen Mag's dad would have him dropping cars off at different locations and then driving back in others. All he was ever told was: 'never look in the trunk' and he never had. The money he was earning by driving cars was way better than his allowance so he didn't mind at all. The job made him feel like he was important, like a man.

They were on the second floor sitting in front of the massive television, quiet, lights low, both collecting themselves. Mag knew that he had to try to help her see that the events of her past were taking her future hostage just as she trad been taken as a little girl.

Mag thought back to five years ago to a youngster whose name he remembered was Jason. Jason was fresh in the prison system and the predators had taken him fast. They had beaten him until he learned that giving them what they wanted was easier than the pain. Jason had money and he'd eventually paid the right people for protection. The predators left Jason alone but by that time the fire had burned out of his eyes and he'd lost all motivation to live. Around the same time Mag had just finished a powerful book called 'Man's Search For Meaning' by Viktor E Frankl and he had fell in love with the 'logotherapy' way of healing. Dr. Frankl describes the role of a logotherapist's role consisting of: "widening and broadening the visual field of the patient so that the whole spectrum of potential meaning becomes conscious and visible to him." Mag saw the power in giving pain and suffering a meaning so that men and women could persevere in spite of pain towards the purpose of their lives.

Mag hated to see youngsters with so much potential just ruin their lives. Jason was just a short timer too, two years and he was home. Mag started working with Jason showing him how his pain could be a source that showed him his personal strength and could lead to him helping to liberate others who have suffered the same way as himself. Mag gave him personal testimony of how trials and tribulations contributed to his own growth mentally and emotionally in union with his higher power. Mag showed Jason a quote that was one of his favorites by William James that said: 'The greatest discovery of my generation is that human beings can alter their lives by altering their attitudes."

Mag knew he had to find a way to teach Josh that progress involves risk. You can't steal second base and keep your foot on first.

"Your higher power has a purpose for what you went through, Jason. It's up to you to dig into the pain and allow him to show you," Mag remembered telling Josh.

"Where the hell was this higher power when these fools took turns on me every other day, huh?" Josh had asked.

"He was the same place he was when they beat Jesus over and over again, and just like him your pain has a purpose too. Bro, I know you are hurting and feel lost, but perspective can save you. Turn your shit into fertilizer, J!"

Mag remembered Josh looking deep into his eyes in that moment. It was like he was searching for hope in what Mag was telling him, looking for a 'why' to his suffering. Three weeks later, Jason jumped off three row head first and broke his neck. He died instantly.

For a week Mag walked around in his own fog. He thought about what more he could have done. He soul-searched his own pain and realized that Jason's death had a meaning for him. Not all can be saved. When a man or woman loses their will to live, no words can save them. In the end one had to grieve and move on with the lesson.

Now he sat beside Jasmine. He hadn't chosen to get involved in her emotional issues this deep, but nevertheless he was involved and if he could leave tonight having helped her see things differently then he knew he could leave in total peace. For everything she'd done for him thus far, he felt he at least owed her that.

He could tell that she was waiting for him to say something. She had slipped off her heels and had her legs curled up under her, mascara trails lined her face. Mag waited for the energy in the room to shift down a bit.

Jasmine said, "I know."

"If you knew better you'd do better, Jasmine! That stunt could have cost me and you our freedom and we still don't know if someone got your license plate number or if that establishment had cameras. That shit was impulsive and dumb as shit!" Mag wasn't overly angry. He was more frustrated than angry for he understood what lay beneath her actions. He still knew he had to be firm.

Mag said, "Right here, right now, while in this emotional state, I'm going to have you go back to the darkness of your abduction and tell me exactly what happened so that I can in turn to do my best to understand and help."

She was shaking her head back and forth. She folded her arms, tears already starting to form, threatening to spill.

"No! I won't go back there. It's too painful," She said.

"Look me in my eyes when I speak to you." Mag said.

She turned her body on the sofa towards his direction. A tear fell from her left eye. He chose not to wipe it. Scott Peck M.D. once said: 'the tendency to avoid problems and emotional suffering within the souls of people is the primary basis of all mental illness.' Mag could see that she was caught up and infected with this same illness.

Mag said, "Hoping that their issues will somehow go away they ignore the tornado warring within. They try to forget the past to the point of pretending that it doesn't exist. They take pills and drugs so that in deadening themselves to the pain, they attempt to drown out the issues that are internally eating them alive. Do you follow me so far, J?"

She was focused on Mag as if she was starving for answers. She didn't speak but just nodded her head up and down, acknowledging that she understood.

Mag continued, "The drugs become a sub for the pain. Relationships are used to drown out the emptiness. Even sex is a cover for absent emotional satisfaction. Believe it or not Jasmine, 70% of all young girls who are sexually abused or molested in turn become prostitutes or openly promiscuous."

"Why?" Jasmine asked, her voice soft.

"Well, by giving of their bodies at will they feel they can take back power that was stolen from them as young women. Another side of that same coin is what is called 'starvation economies' in where the victimization leads to the abused overly clinging to things that make them feel safe and love because of what was taken or just 'not having enough' when they were young."

"How do you know these things?" Jasmine asked.

"I've always been intrigued with what makes people tick and began to read up on the subject while in prison. I used myself to test the things that I was reading and if the spirit confirmed something I made it wisdom that I lived by and helped others with. By doing this I learned that my 'gift' was discernment. I am able to feel people, understand their darkness, and help them use it to find purpose."

"I don't want to go back there Mag. I'm scared." Jasmine said, her voice almost childlike. Mag could see the fear in her eyes, her hands were visibly shaking.

"How about I hold you in these arms as you go back to that scary place and tell me what happened." Mag said.

Jasmine hesitated for a second, then slid to his end of the sectional couch. She placed her back against his chest, laying her head back onto his left shoulder. She closed her eyes and took the long journey back to Mexico, back into the darkness.

Mag felt her body begin to shake. The room was cool, the light sweat that was forming on her head had nothing to do with the temp.

"It's okay. I got you. Tell me what you see." Mag said. "Remember, I'm there with you this time."

Mag wrapped his arms around her. She held onto his arms like the safety bar on a carnival ride.

She began, "Ok, uh, I'm in between two of them. They just took me from school. They are speaking in a hurried tone, telling me that my dad has arranged for them to pick me up. They say it's an emergency and we have to hurry."

"I asked the man to my left 'Is my dad ok?' and he just smiles at me. He has stained yellow teeth with a gold cap over his left front tooth.

Jasmine was speaking very slowly. Mag occasionally wiped tears from her eyes.

"It's ok. Keep going." Mag said.

"It's hot in the car. The air coming through the window isn't helping at all. We turned onto a dirt road. I can tell by the way the car is rocking from side to side, and I can hear the crunch of the tires against gravel. We're pulling into a village. I see men milling around with big guns. I know something is extremely wrong when Mr. Gold Tooth pulls me out of the car by my hair."

Jasmine's voice was cracking and she was trembling. Mag had to focus to hear her words. He held her a little tighter.

"I'm kicking and screaming, scratching at his hands, yelling for my dad. He pulls me into a shed. I scoot along the dirt floor to the far left corner. He shuts the door and locks it. I'm, I'm in the corner now. I'm hugging my knees tight, crying. The only light coming into the shed is coming through the cracks in the wood. The smell of the room makes me throw up. It smells of animals, urine, and feces. The only other thing in the room with me is a stained white bucket with flies buzzing over the top. I'm walking towards it."

Mag noticed her shoulders start to heave and her cry became audible.

"It's ok, it's ok. I'm in there with you." Mag said, "Tell me what you see."

"I look into the bucket out of curiosity. I look in and I see, I see fingers and toes."

Mag began to rub her arms to soothe her cry.

She continued, "I run back to my corner. I'm calling for my dad over and over again. Didn't he love me? Why wasn't he coming? I must have cried myself to sleep or maybe it wasn't a dream but what I'm about to tell you felt so real. A figure stood before me. He was gold with black chains wrapped all around his body. He spoke and said his name was Kalenjin. He said that he knew that I was afraid and that my fear is what drew him to me. He said that if I would go into my fear, my pain, and into the darkness that he could show me my strength. He said that I could grow from this experience only if I took his hand. He said to trust him. He extended his hand and I withdrew. I didn't trust anyone. I was so scared. I ran to the other side of the room and tucked my head between my knees. When I looked up the figure was gone."

Mag felt Jasmine take a deep breath. She continued.

"The next morning I'm startled awake by Gold Tooth and he has two apples and a bottle of water. I'm so hungry, Mag. He walks into the room and sets the water and fruit down. He walks back to the door, pokes his head out, looks around, and comes back in.

He said, "If you want to eat, if you ever want to see your dad again, you'll give me what I want!"

"I can tell by the look in his eyes what he wants, Mag. I was only twelve but I was a smart girl."

Mag could see the whole scene in his head. His punches and kicks are going right through Gold Tooth like in the movie 'Ghost'. He feels so angry. He's holding her so tight.

"It's ok, Jasmine. I'm with you. Face your fears." Mag feels her take in another deep breath, drawing in courage from his words and his arms around her.

"The entire next week is just a blur. He took my soul from me. My mind and body were numb. I went to a place far away from that little room so that I didn't have to face the things he did to me."

Mag hadn't noticed the tears in his own eyes until he felt the warm water on his face.

Jasmine said, "After a week or so they put me in the car to drive me to my dad. I hardly noticed. I was in a daze. My dad's voice brought me back from that far away place. I cried in his arms and held on tight, never wanting to let go, holding on for my life to what I loved."

Mag wiped a tear from his eye, then a few from hers.

"What happened after that?" he asked.

"We got home and my dad fed and ran me some fresh bath water. After I had ate and was settled he looked me in my eyes and asked me to be completely honest with him. I told him every-thing. That night after he put me to bed I heard him in the living room cursing, throwing things, and crying. He blamed himself for what happened to me. He was out of his mind with rage and pain. I heard a knock on our front door and my Uncle Torrez walks in with three other men. I'm watching them through the crack in my door. They pass around big guns and knives. They give my dad one, talk for about ten minutes pointing at some kind of map, and then they left in a hurry."

Mag noticed that her breathing had slowed and the tears were drying on her face.

"I was only twelve Mag, but I was smart. I knew what they were about to go do and deep in my soul I have to say I was happy about it. Two or three hours later my dad rushes back into the house and tells me to pack my things. His eyes are wide and wild, almost like he was demon possessed. He tells me that we are going to America to start a new life away from all the drugs and cartel controlled lands. We get a ride to the border. My dad pays a guy to take us the rest of the way and the rest is history. We've been here in San Antonio ever since. We never talk about what happened in Mexico. I hid away the pain and fear of the incident in a deep and dark place within my soul and left it there. It's been buried for 32 years until now."

Mag did the calculations in his mind. If she was 12 when she was taken in Mexico and she'd been carrying it hidden for 32 years now, that would make her 44 years old. She carried her age exceptionally.

"I'm so proud of you, Jasmine." Mag said. He was still holding her in his arms, her head laying back on his shoulders.

He continued, "You had the courage to go back in time to a painful place in your soul and face your pain head on. Believe it or not, that's the first step in healing and realizing how your past is affecting your future, your today."

"You really think what happened to me in Mexico is affecting my life today?" She asked.

"Of course," Mag said, "at an unconscious level we are always seeking to resolve our childhood issues. I don't know him, but I bet your husband was cold and distant, maybe verbally or even physically abusive. You had a strong motivation to change him I bet."

She shot up out of Mag's arms, turned to face him. "How'd you know that?" She asked, a puzzled look in her eyes.

"Well, by attracting men similar to the men who oppressed you when you were abused, you are given the chance to heal yourself if only you can change him, make him stop being the way he is, the way you couldn't stop the man who oppressed you in Mexico. Your husband most likely rejected your attempts to change him which resulted in explosive fights between the two of you."

Mag could see that what he was saying was resonating in her spirit. He could see her replaying the arguments and fights in her mind.

He continued, "Most likely you seduced him, whenever you knew you would see him your clothes were subtle, sexy, innocent, and pretty; but also sheer and close-fitting. You didn't make him wait long. In order to get your power back from what was taken from you in childhood, you've learned to use sex as a weapon."

Jasmine stood up, anger in her eyes. Mag was confused. He was only trying to help.

She said, "You don't know me! You can't judge me!"

Mag was caught off guard and remembered reading some-where that therapists sometimes withheld information from a patient because they were not ready to deal with what was really hiding in their soul motivating their actions.

"I was only trying to help you connect your past to what is going on in your life right now. I know hearing this information and going back to that darkness is painful, but I truly meant no disrespect, Jasmine. That is not who I am."

They stood looking at each other as if in a western standoff.

She said, "I know your type, Mag. I can see right through you, sir. You're the type of man who acts as if he has it all together and is always giving out advice to cover up his own lack of self confidence by assuming the position of the wise man. Keep your damn advice because I don't need it!"

She stormed upstairs. Mag heard her bedroom door slam. He sat back down and leaned his head back on the sectional. Mag understood his mistake and understood that the truth is a little too much for some people. He remembered reading about a man who went to a psychologist over some strange dreams he was having. When the psychiatrist told him that he was subconscious-ly dealing with thoughts of homosexual tendencies the man stormed out of the office never to be seen again for treatment.

Maybe before he left in the morning he could make amends and leave her with a few words of encouragement.

He stood, stretched, then went to his room and undressed.

"What a hell of a first day out, Mag," he said to the room. He set the bedside alarm for 8:00 AM. He was excited to spend time with Stacy. He slid under the covers feeling like he'd helped Jasmine more than he'd hurt her.

Boy was he wrong!

Chapter 10: The Dream

The softness of the mattress had Mag in a deep sleep. He awoke with a start. Jasmine was straddling him naked with tears in her eyes. Her arms are raised high above her head, a huge knife in her hands. Her eyes have a wildness to them mixed in with a look of anger, pain, and fury.

Mag recognized the knife from hunting magazines he used to borrow from one of his celly's who hunted game professionally before turning his skill into hunting human game. The knife was made by the Blackhawk company. It was called The Gideon Tanto. The five inch fixed blade had a tanto design; the full design is good for piercing and slashing, not a good thing for Mag at the moment. For some reason Mag remembered that the handle was made of CNC machine textured G10 with two holes in the blade for easy puncturing. Mag even remembered the damn price of the weapon, $129.

"I don't understand why you don't want me." Jasmine said in tears. One of Mag's hands was pinned down by Jasmine's knee, his other hand he used as a makeshift shield to cover his face and chest.

He said, "Calm down. Let's talk about this Jasmine. You don't want to do this. Put the knife down baby."

"We talked enough last night when you judged me and called me a damn whore. I'm going to show you what happens to people who feel they know it all." Jasmine said.

She still had the knife raised over her head.

Mag said, "Beautiful, I would never disrespect you. Remember how I encouraged you outside the prison, how I held you in my arms as you cried? I've only loved on you since we met, Jasmine. Put the knife down and let's talk about this. Please, Jasmine."

"I killed my husband, and now I'll kill you!"

The knife came down with lightning speed. It punctured Mag's left lung. He started to choke on his own blood as she stabbed him again. . .

Mag woke with a start, and jumped out of the bed right as Jasmine walked into the room.

"Surprise!" She was holding a set of keys in one hand and an envelope in the other. Mag was still trying to catch his breath. His heart was thumping a million miles a minute. He looked over at the clock. It was already 12:00 AM. He had set the alarm for 8:00 AM. He wondered why it hadn't gone off. He figured that it being his first night on a real soft and comfortable bed may have had something to do with it.

"Surprise? What's with the keys and the envelope?" Mag asked.

"Well," she started, "I was laying in bed last night after I stormed out on you and I was feeling bad for the way I spoke to you. I realized after thinking that you really care about me and want the best for me."

Mag was still waiting for the answer to his question while also trying to calm himself from the dream.

She continued, "I feel so at peace now that you went back with me to that terrible place from my past. In your arms I feel the same I felt in my father's arms the morning after everything happened to me, and I never want to treat you the way I did again. We faced my fears together and I feel so much better."

Mag instantly realized his mistake. When he took her back to that dark place to face her fears, he was supposed to show her that her 'higher power' was the one holding her through the entire experience and not him. She was supposed to now understand that God would always be with her through anything that she faced, not him. She was now that much more dependent on him and it would be hard for him to leave without her feeling abandoned or unsafe. 'How can I fix this?' He thought to himself.

Jasmine said, "I wanted to find a way to thank you for what you have meant to my life thus far and I remembered you saying something about your dream car while we were eating. You said you wanted an old-school Eldog drop-top Cadillac."

She had a huge grin on her face. Mag couldn't believe what he was hearing. He could feel the adrenaline building in his stomach.

"Well I got up this morning, found exactly what you wanted on the internet, mint condition, and went and paid for it in cash just to show you how much you mean to me Mag!"

Before he realized what he was doing he was jumping up and down and hugging Jasmine. He broke the embrace and looked her in her eyes, no recollection of the dream remaining.

He said, "You got to be kidding me, girl. I'm speechless. What can I say? I mean. . ."

Mag took the envelope from her and opened it. It was the title with his name on it.

"Wow, you didn't have to." He walked over to the window and looked out. Where is it? I gots to lay my eyes on it!"

"I remembered you saying that you wanted it a certain color and so I had it dropped off at a great custom paint shop and they are going to paint it two-tone Dallas Cowboy's grey and blue. They said it should be ready in about two or three days!"

Mag was smiling but his heart had dropped. He heard something in his spirit say, 'The cheese is your weakness! How much cheese does a mouse get to eat before the trap snaps?'

She handed him the keys to his Cadillac and a cell phone.

She said, "They will call you on this phone when they are on the way to drop it off."

'Two or three more days, what am I going to do? If I refuse the gift she will have a meltdown, even more now than before.' He still had the half fake smile on his face.

"Thank you so much for your generosity. I'm overwhelmed." Mag said as a flood of mixed emotions attacked his mind.

"It's the least I can do for the peace you have given my soul."

Mag thought fast, "Look, today I'm going out and about. I got some biz that I got to handle. I don't know how long I'll be gone so don't wait up for me, alright?"

She had an instant frown on her face, "Why don't I take you around? I don't mind, really Mag. I don't. I know you really don't know your way around."

Mag said, "I really need to do this by myself, alright? This will give us some time to miss each other."

"But I wanted to go horseback riding with you today, Mag. I own three horses."

Mag said, "That's cool. If I get back in time we'll do that. If not let's do it tomorrow. We got three days to kill right?"

"How will you get around?" She asked.

"The bus."

"That's unacceptable for a man of your stature Mag. At least take my husband's old car. It's in the garage with the keys in it. Hopefully it has gas. It hasn't been driven in forever."

"Alright, alright, I'll do that. I'm about to go bathe and get ready. And again, thank you so much for my dream car. I really don't know what to say or do to make you understand." Mag gave her a hug and a kiss on the cheek.

"When you get back I got some ideas on how you can thank me," Jasmine said with a sly smile.

Mag didn't respond but just headed into the bathroom to start the shower. He was excited to spend the day with Stacy. They say hindsight is twenty-twenty.

Chapter 11: The Zoo

Mag exited the shower feeling physically rejuvenated but a mental unrest was a small presence at the back of his mind. He felt as though his freedom was trapped behind a wall made up of his care and concern for Jasmine. When he was done dressing he looked at his watch realizing that it was already 2:20 in the afternoon.

He pulled out the cell phone that Jasmine had given him and called Stacy. A mental fight ensued while the phone rang; he was a grown ass man and shouldn't have to lock the bathroom door just to have a conversation! The other side swung back with a vicious left hook by playing the scene out in his mind: Jasmine walks in excited, asks who he's talking to, "a friend," Stacy asked who 'that' is, "a friend" . . . "I'm a little more than a friend Jasmine teases Mag by twerking. . . "I'm going to let you handle your biz Mag," Stacy says and hangs up the phone. Mag got up and locked the door. His goal was to get through these last few days with as less drama as possible.

The thump of his heart sped up just a notch as the phone rang its familiar song.

"Hello? This better be you Mag or you're in trouble boy."

Mag laughed into the phone. Her voice fit exactly how she looked, seductive. Mag loved how her energy made him feel. His spirit hummed when he connected with her.

"Damn girl, what if I was your boss or something? I wouldn't be the only one in trouble." Mag said.

"Caller ID my best friend and besides I don't have anything else in the world to do today but you."

"You promise." Mag said.

"Boy get your head out the gutter."

"No, it's definitely in the clouds when it comes to you and the way I feel when we are connecting. I can't explain it but my spirit feels a certain joy when I see your face in my mind's eye."

"Awww, that's so sweet Mag. I laid up thinking about you the other night trying to figure out the exact feeling that you just explained. You feel so natural to me. There's a flow with us." She said.

"Most definitely Stacy, I agree. I'm excited to see you. Shoot your address and I'm on my way going ninety miles an hour the whole way."

She laughed, "Okay, I just texted you the address. Did you get it?"

Mag looked down at the phone and opened the received text, "Got it beautiful, I'm on my way. Make sure you're wearing that radient smile I love."

"Got you, and make sure you wear some comfortable shoes. I got something nice planned," Stacy said.

"I'll call you when I'm out front." Mag hung up the phone and noticed a shadow move from under the bedroom door. The thump in his chest revved up a notch. He heard receding footsteps. "Damn," he heard himself say out loud. He cursed half because he didn't know how much the person heard, and half because of the inner battle of feeling bound by an invisible emotional obligation that he didn't sign up for.

Mag listened harder. The sound of steps had stopped. He unlocked the door and opened it. He checked his pockets for his wallet and descended the stairs.

His right ear drum vibrated and he turned his head towards the direction of the kitchen. He heard a noise that sounded like a door sliding shut. Mag entered the massive kitchen decorated in black marble counter tops outlined with stainless steel handles and knobs. Mag noticed a sliding glass door that lead to a patio. He slid the door open. The air was fresh and cool against his face reminding him once again of the freedom that was at last his, 'why did he have to be reminded' he wondered. What was it that was holding him in this self imposed prison? One part of his mind said it was his heart. A small voice screamed from somewhere deep: the cheese is your weakness!

Mag took a deep breath and inhaled the 85 degree weather into his lungs. The sky seemed to smile down on him through the scattered clouds. In the distance he noticed Jasmine walking along a stone path that lead towards the huge log cabin that she said her father lived in. Mag remembered their encounter, the dark eyes, "She's not like other women". . .

Even from a distance Mag could see that the cabin was made out of strong cedar or oak wood, trees that had gained their strength through age and endurance. Jasmine was walking in a hurried pace. Mag wondered what she had heard through the door.

Mag found his way through the house and into the garage. What he found parked next to Jasmine's BMW made his heart drop and his mouth open. The pearl white '05 Phantom Rolls Royce was immaculate. The top was down with the keys in the ignition. White candy pearl paint, white seats, white on white, suicide doors, he was in a dream. He walked around the car in circles allowing his fingers to slide along the car. If he woke up in his bunk at that very moment he might just end it all, he jokingly thought.

He checked the tags and registration. They were legit. He slid into the driver's seat and checked his Rolex. It was almost three. He had to get going.

Mag hit the garage door opener and the radiant sunlight flooded in illuminating the Phantom. He started the engine, smooth. He felt presidential in the seats. He opened the phone and put Stacy's address into the GPS system. He turned the radio dial to 105.7 and the song 'Good Luck Charm' by Jagged Edge was just getting started. Mag pulled out of the garage feeling like a king. He closed the garage door behind him singing along with the song, "and you always got some sexy underwear on. Something good has come my way, since you came in my life." Mag wasn't the best singer but he could hold a note.

The Phantom Double R seemed to float over the street. His lion pinky ring was blinding in the sunlight. The Rolex seemed as if it was in competition with the ring. Mag let them fight.

Every time Mag stopped at a light people watched him. He wondered what they would think if they knew just twenty four hours ago he was sleeping in a prison cell with his shirt as his pillow. Out in the world, just him and the open road, his dream. He felt powerful in the moment, blessed, while at the same time feeling a conditioned peace, a borrowed triumph. From his subconscious there came a sequence of words, like a strange disembodied oracle from deep within: Mouse Trap! The cheese is your weakness! How much cheese does a mouse get to eat before the trap snaps him?

"I really don't give a damn!" Mag was surprised at his response to the inner voice. He was just feeling too damn good at the moment. He wasn't about to let some weird ass voice steal his blessing.

Mag checked his watch as he pulled up to the curb. It was 3:19. "Fashionably late," he thought, smiling. He put the car in park but left it running. It was full of gas.

Stacy must of hard him pull up because after a quick minute she stepped out and gave the radiance of the sun a run for its money. As Mag stepped out of the car and struggled to keep his manhood from rising. A nervous excitement filled his chest cavity as he watched her dance her movements, "Wow," he said as he held the passenger door open for her.

Stacy made casual wear look formal. The Jordan Air Force Ones, the best of both worlds, make her look like she could moon walk. The blue jean denim skirt stopped mid-thigh, creating wonder and anticipation with every step. The plain white t-shirt with the spurs logo on it looked like it came from Macy's the way she wore it. She looked remarkable.

"Close your mouth boy," she said, "you don't look too bad yourself." Her eyes were stunning in the light. They had Mag lost in their world, hypnotized in their array of colors. Mag shook free of the trance as he closed the door behind her.

Mag noticed her rubbing the soft leather in the Double R and nodding her head to that 'Dirty' by Tank. Mag felt that gravitational pull again in his chest. The natural joy that came from being close to her, her presence made everything feel better. She winked at Mag as she sang along with the jam.

Mag said, "Okay! I see you can hold a tune. You got a lil something-something."

"You should hear ya girl in the shower. My other self tells me I sound like Queen B," she said smiling. She turned down the music.

"First you at the gas station in the Beamer, and now you pull up in the Phantom . . . the FED's ain't gonna pull us over on the highway are they?" she asked, laughing.

"I got six keys in the trunk ma. If they ask make sure you own up to your shit too," Mag said. She hit him in the arm.

He said, "Naw ma, Gods been good to me and I only pull out the best for the best. By the way, where is my hug at?"

She smiled that radiant smile and leaned over in her seat. Her smell was warm somehow, fresh like a spring flower. Her body felt so natural in his arms. Mag allowed his inner heat to escape through his mouth to find a resting place on her neck. He felt her purr. He instantly knew this was one of her spots. When they released their embrace both noticed the chill bumps on the others arms. They smiled a knowing look in their eyes of how the night would end.

He said, "So where we off to beautiful?"

She got excited, "Okay, so I hope you like animals because we're headed to the historical San Antonio zoo."

It was Mag's turn to be excited, "I love animals, especially big cats. I knew there was a reason I liked you the first moment I saw you."

Mag put the car in drive and pulled out. He turned the music back up and Avant was telling some girl how he could read her mind.

They pulled into the zoo's parking lot at 4:00. She took charge and took Mag's hand into hers. It felt like he was holding heaven.

Mag felt in step with peace, his steps were light. It seemed as if he were moving in slow motion, freedom attained. She moved in closer and hugged his arm as they strolled. The smiles on the little kids' faces warmed Mag's heart. Pure joy, the pressures of life absent from their souls, they jumped and twirled with anticipation. Their mother and father watched them with pride in their eyes.

As they waited in line Mag noticed a colorful sign announcing that the zoo had been operating for over 100 years. He noticed that admission was $12 for adults. He pulled out his wallet.

"Put that back. Are you crazy Mag? You are my guest and I'm paying," she said, "you can get us snacks inside."

"You're a rare breed of woman, Stacy, a rare breed. But you slick too because you know you damn well a drink is probably $12 and food $15," Mag said smiling.

"Boy," she hit his arm again smiling back.

Mag noticed that the zoo closed at 6:00 PM. He checked his watch. It was 4:30. They had an hour and a half to enjoy themselves.

"Welcome to the historical San Antonio Zoo. We hope you enjoy your time with us," a bubbly lady said as they entered. She handed them a pamphlet.

"I'm trying to go see the big cats ASAP." Mag said.

Stacy was beaming, "You're like a kid in a candy store Mag. Come this way. I'm taking you to a place called Africa Live Exhibit," she said as she pulled the camera out of her purse.

The sun was low in the sky. The air was cool and refreshing. Mag took in the moment for all the men that he knew would never again experience free society, men who in one moment of heated passion had lost it all. One moment in exchange for a lifetime.

"Look," Mag said, "is that a hippo? That is one." Mag answered his own question.

Stacy was busy snapping pictures, "Okay move right here. I want to get a pic of you with it in the background. . . Okay, got it."

They continued to walk down the path. Mag felt an alert move his spirit but couldn't put his finger on it. He shook it off. Inside another enclosure Mag saw a huge Nile crocodile slide into the water, maybe trying to creep up on unsuspecting prey.

"Look Mag, look!" Stacy said as she pulled him to the other side of the walkway.

The tiger was massive. He looked like he weighed at least five hundred pounds.

"Isn't he so majestic?" Stacy said.

"Yes he is ma, and I'm so glad they have the zoo set up like this because if they didn't and he came charging at us I'd throw you in front and run," Mag said smiling. She chased Mag in circles with her arms raised.

"You violent," Mag said. She just shook her head.

They walked down a little more and right there in front of their eyes was the king. His mane was full and golden brown. He was full grown, the grace in his steps magnificent.

Mag was holding Stacy from behind taking in the beauty of the moment, the energy between them creating their own force field of passion. The python began to stir. There was no way she didn't feel him waking. She didn't move. She had her harms up over her head, interlocked behind his neck. His arms were around her waist. They stood like that watching the king do his thing. He could stay in that moment forever.

An older couple passing by noticed them. The way they moved together one could tell had come from many years in bond. The woman gave them a thumbs up.

"Ma'am," Stacy said, "do you mind taking a picture for us?"

"No, not at all. The love that ya'll share has to be captured and remembered for a lifetime."

After two poses Mag said, "Let's take one touching lips."

"You think you slick don't you?" Stacy said.

Mag just grinned. They puckered their lips and touched them together. Electricity! The older lady cleared her throat, "Okay." But they didn't hear a word. The dance of kissing came back natural with her. All was forgotten in that moment. Her taste and feel was all that mattered. They would have devoured one another if the lady hadn't broken their trance by tapping on Mag's shoulder.

"Um, sorry ma'am, sir," Mag said to the couple, "no disrespect."

"None taken son," the man said and winked as if to say 'I was young once'.

Mag and Stacy both looked embarrassed. They told the couple thanks and walked off. By the time they left the African Life they had pictures of African wild dogs, monkeys, zebras, and elephants.

When they stopped to get a quick snack, Mag had a nagging feeling that they were being followed. He looked behind them to his left and his right, nil. He shook it off.

"Before we leave I want to take you to one of my favorite places here," Stacy said.

Right next door to the African Live was a place called Lory Landing. They entered the area and Mag loved how they had created an open air environment. The place had large colorful birds flying around everywhere. One parakeet looking bird flew right at Mag. He tried to duck it but it perched right on top of his head.

"Ahhh, get it, get it, it's trying to bite me!" Mag said.

Stacy laughed so hard she could barely get her words out, "Be still scary cat, they're friendly."

Mag stopped moving but was tense. He was sweating and the bird started to lick his sweat.

"What, what the hell!"

"They like the salt in human sweat. Calm down. It's okay." She said. She was still giggling as she took the camera from Mag and took pictures of the bird on top of his head. "Instant classic," she smiled.

Stacy held a finger out to the bird and it climbed on. She had a cup of nectar that the bird immediately started to eat. The bird had beautiful colors: a red curved beak, green feathers lead up to a purple head. Its eyes were red around the outside and jet black in the middle.

After the nectar was gone the bird flew off.

"That's what you get punk. He was just using you for your nectar," Mag said.

"I don't blame him. My nectar is sweet," she replied with a wink. The way she said it was like a song by Jill Scott. She added, "The nights still young my friend, the nights still young.

The comment gave Mag hope that the night would end in his favor.

She said, "And now before we leave I have to show you who Thelma and Louise are."

Mag couldn't believe his eyes. Thelma and Louise was a two-headed turtle. "I read about shit like this, but wow. It really does happen."

She said, "It's the result of twin embryos that didn't quite separate completely but continued to develop, resulting in fully formed and functioning heads on a single body. Cool, huh?"

"Can I touch them?" Mag asked.

"Yeah, go ahead. Just be gentle. Although uncommon, they appear healthy. They enjoy meals and you won't believe this, they even have their own Facebook page," Stacy said. Mag took a picture.

"Please begin the exit the zoo. We are now closing. We hope you enjoyed your time here. Please come back soon." A deep voice said over an invisible intercom.

"Awww, I was having so much fun," Stacy said laying her head on Mag's chest and wrapping her arms around him.

He said, "The nights still young my friend, the nights still young." Mag winked his eye. She just smiled a smile that seemed to say that she agreed.

Mag held her tight as they made their way back to the car. He held joy within his soul in contrast to what he had endured the last nineteen years of his life. He held out hope that those who deserved it would get their chance when their time came. He held a smile on his face.

"Thank you so much for that Stacy, I really enjoyed myself. You were enjoying yourself a little too much when that bird flew on my damn head."

She burst out laughing, "Ain't my fault you scary, but you're welcome Mag. I enjoyed myself too."

It was 6:15 and the sun drowsy and yawning, an indication that it was about to go down for the night.

They got in the car. Mag turned the key over and Usher was telling a story about being in a drop top with a pretty girl next to him.

Mag looked over feeling in tune with the now, the energy of the moment, thankfulness his aura. "So where to now love?" He asked.

She didn't answer right away. She turned towards Mag in her seat looking deep into his eyes as if she were trying to decide something. Mag used his eyes as lasers sending her beams of passion, intimacy, and intention. It had been nineteen years since these emotions had come to visit him. He embraced them with full openness making sure they knew how much he had missed them; he was focused on presenting a controlled hunger verses starvation, spiritual ecstasy verses barbaric desires.

"Are you hungry?" She asked.

"Starving, those little snacks did nothing for me. I need something fulfilling." Mag answered.

"What do you have a taste for?" She asked.

Mag let his gaze slip unconsciously over her body and back up to her eyes. He licked his lips.

She moaned the words, "Stop playing Mag," as if she was having an inner fight that was about to consume her. "For real, what do you want to eat?"

"Okay, it's been a while since I had some home cooking. A nice home cooked dinner. You know how to cook?"

"What? Boy, I can throw down in the kitchen. I am half black."

"Well what are we waiting on?" Mag started the Phantom, "What you know about this?" He turned it up. Trey Songz felt the same way he did. After nineteen years she was gone think he invented sex too.

CHAPTER 12: THE FIRST TIME

They pulled up to the modest one story brick home at fifteen minutes to seven. The inside of her home felt clean, organized, and smelled of vanilla. It allowed you to feel her energy, her style. Mag felt instantly at home and comfortable. Behind a bar sat a tidy kitchen with impeccable wood floors. A hallway off to the right lead to two bedrooms and a master bath.

"Wow, this is nice, Stacy. The Spurs paying you good ma."

"Thank you. Make yourself at home. It won't take me long to whip this up. I got you." She said with a wink and handed him a remote control to the 65" flat screen.

Mag smiled as he flipped through the channels. So much content vying for ones attention. Entertainment for those who balance their time wisely but rocking those to sleep who depend on it to pass time because of a lack of vision.

Mag started to smell the familiar aroma of fried chicken coming from the kitchen. His stomach did a dance called the rumble and then rolled with it. Stacy came in the living room holding a cold glass of iced tea wearing an apron that said 'can you smell what the Stace is cooking'. Mag said thank you and smiled. On her way back to the kitchen she glanced over her shoulder and caught Mag looking at her gift from God. She just smiled.

Mag felt like royalty. A quick sadness shot through his gut for his boys in prison with all that time, sitting in those 6x9 cells away from family, friends, kids, and the love and softness of a woman; maybe for the rest of their lives. Mag would eat this first home cooked meal for those men and if the night got as good as he hoped it would, he would give Stacy the thrill of her life for all those who couldn't. He would accept her gift with intense appreciation making sure that she understood that giving in essence is the nature of receiving.

The vibration of the cell phone in his pocket shook him from his thoughts. Jasmine's face filled the screen. He thought about answering it but decided against it. Too much explaining would have to be done and if Stacy walked in on the conversation it might ruin the magic of their day thus far. Mag pressed the red ignore button. Fifteen seconds later it vibrated again and a text message came through: You been gone all day Mag, are you okay, did something happen, do I need to come and get you? I'm worried, call me when you can.

Mag message back: I'm good, I'm good, nothing to worry about beautiful. Caught up with an old friend of mine and we kickin it. Don't wait up.

Mag turned his phone off. No outside energy would be allowed to enter this moment.

From the left side of his peripheral vision he saw a shadow move across the living room front window. He glanced in that direction. Whatever it was had just flashed across then it was gone. Mag opened the front door and walked onto the front porch, looked left then right, nil.

"Is everything alright?" Stacy said from somewhere behind him.

He walked in and closed the door behind him. She was standing in the archway of the kitchen wiping her hands on a towel.

"Everything's cool," Mag said, "thought about putting the top up on my ride but looking at the neighborhood it feels safe."

"You should be good for the night." Stacy said.

"Who said I'm spending the night," Mag said jokingly.

Stacy just walked off smiling and said, "Come on, foods ready. We're eating out on my back patio."

Mag made sure that the front door was locked, the feeling from the zoo had tried to creep back into his mind but he shook it off and focused on the blessings before him.

On an elegant glass table set for two she had two candles lit. Jazz music played softly through an invisible surround sound speaker. The night air was cool and comfortable. The sun was fully asleep now, no longer fighting its drowsiness. Mag inhaled a deep lung full of the moment. It tasted like freedom.

Mag pulled a chair out for her and she sat down. "Thank you," she said, "you're such a gentleman."

Mag sat across from her, "No, thank you. You're such a gentlewoman. Look at this food girl."

Fried chicken, mashed potatoes, corn, green beans, and corn bread adorned the plate. They said grace then dug in.

"I feel so comfortable with you Stacy. You feel so natural to me. I don't feel that you'll judge me when I say that I spent the last nineteen years of my life in prison, and if tonight is what it's all lead to, then I must say that it was well worth it."

Stacy dropped the drumstick she was eating and jumped up from the table, "You have to leave and right now! Get out!"

"Woah, woah, woah. Calm down, calm down Stacy. Let me explain."

She burst out laughing, "You should have seen your face." She was holding her stomach she was laughing so hard. Mag threw a piece of corn at her and it hit her in the shoulder.

"Oh, so you're a part time cheerleader slash comedian huh?" Mag said, laughing himself.

"So what did you do, like murder someone or something?"

"Damn so you just jump right to the worst," Mag said laughing. "I was 18 years old, very adventurous, a very inquisitive mind. I've always had a soft spot for other people's pain. One day I'm walking through my apartment and I pass a sliding glass door that's open. I look inside just curious and see a slim white lady sitting on her couch holding her right eye and crying. Instinctively I poke my head in and ask her if she's ok. She looks up at me and she has blood on her lip and a black eye. She shakes her head no, she wasn't alright. I ask her if she needs help on if she wanted me to dial 911. This question made her cry even harder. I should have left but I didn't. Hindsight is 20/20. I step inside unconsciously and tell her to calm down and that everything was going to be alright. Her apartment smelled of fear, anger, violence, and it looked as though a tornado had blown through it."

Stacy was taking bites of her food, listening intently.

"Tables were overturned, dishes were broken, pictures torn from the walls, fist sized holes everywhere, it was a mess. I asked her again if she wanted me to call the police and she said no, he'd kill her if she did. As soon as she said that her front door flew open and this big white guy storms in smelling like three day old beer and cigs. He asks me what the hell I'm doing with his lady. He can barely keep his balance. 'Nothing sir' I tell him. I guess he doesn't believe me because he charges me full force. Right then I threw the hardest wild right hook I've ever thrown in my life and it lands flush against his chin. It stops him dead in his tracks. His body straightens and he falls straight back and hits his head on something that penetrates his skull."

"Did he die?" Stacy asked.

"The lady starts screaming, 'you killed my husband, you killed my husband you black fucker!' I run out of her house a hundred miles an hour. A couple days later the police come to my school and take me and some other boys who look like me down to the station and put us through a line-up. She picks me right out, says

I trashed her house, beat her up because she wouldn't have sex with me and when her husband walked in on us I assaulted him which lead to his death."

"Oh my God Mag, that's crazy. What happened next?"

"Well, as you can imagine I'm in shock. They charge me with murder. The only thing that saved me is her violent history with him and a neighbor who heard everything through the walls and testified on my behalf."

"Well why'd you still end up in prison?" She asked.

"They still charged me with man-slaughter. I had a court appointed lawyer. They gave me nineteen years and made me do the whole sentence."

"Wow," she said, "What was prison like?"

"My homeboys King B and Buddy Love wrote a whole book about prison life called 'Escaping the Pen'. I could write a book on the subject myself but in a nutshell: only the strong survive. Not so much in a physical way but it's the mind that I speak of. Being surrounded by so much negative energy and oppression, men lose their minds and sense of direction. They become one with the darkness."

"Sounds tough," she said.

"I learned a lot about myself, my strength and weakness. All that time with yourself in those cells you have no choice but to face yourself and the many demons you have buried."

"Well how'd you make it?" she asked, "What was your drive?"

"I determined early that I was going to focus on three areas of my life: mind, body and spirit. Mentally I made a decision to learn. Every day I strived to learn not only educational knowledge but I was determined to learn who I was. Physically I worked out every day. I felt I was a king and so if I wanted to feel like one I had to look like one. Last but not least, I focused on a relationship outside of religion with the Creator. If I planted a seed each day in each of these areas then I knew that I had done my time and not merely passed it. Overall I think I came out pretty well," Mag smiled.

"I think I would have to second that." She said.

Things went quiet while they finished their meal. Each bite exploded in his mouth with flavors that he had missed and dreamed about for years. At times she looked up at Mag and smiled, knowing that he was enjoying every bite, a powerful hum vibrated his soul. Mag noticed the smile in her eyes. In giving we also receive, and that was the joy in her eyes that Mag noticed. To be able to cook such a small meal and it mean such a big thing was so amazing. In return Mag was able to give her the simple gift of truly being appreciated.

"Damn girl, you put your foot in this. I tasted a little toe in that last bite," Mag said smiling.

"I do a lil something-something. . . but Mag, ummm, I need to say this and just be straight up. I feel so comfortable with you. You feel so natural to me. I don't feel like you'll judge me when I say that I want to give you tonight all that you have dream of for the last 19 years of your life. I've been celibate for a year because no man has sparked that desire or whom I felt worthy but tonight with you I feel is what I sacrificed for and if you feel the same then it has all been worth it." She seemed like she was holding her breath.

"On our first date!!!" Mag said, "I knew you was a thot, and here I was thinking you was different." Mag stood to leave.

Her mouth was wide open in disbelief. Mag burst out laughing.

"Payback is a bitch. You should have seen your face."

She picked a green bean and threw it. It hit him on his forehead.

"Oh hell naw, you been hitting me all day. It's on," Mag said.

He came around the table. She tried to run. She made it all the way to her bedroom door when Mag caught her from behind and playfully bit her on the back of her neck. Chills shot across her skin instantly. "Umm," she uttered. Mag heard the words to a country song by Billy Currington in his head, 'must be doing something right, I just heard you sigh, lean into my kiss and close those deep blue need you eyes'.

Mag nibbled at the nape of her neck again and ran his hand across her breast. Her nipples were awake, erect, craving for attention. Stacy turned the door handle and they stumbled into the room drunk with passion. The only light in the room was coming from the moon through the bedroom window. It illuminated her skin. Mag was lightly biting and sucking her shoulders, neck, and behind her ears while peeling off her skirt, bra, and shirt. She turned around to face him. Her eyes seemed to be glowing in the moonlight. The volcanic passion that had been building for nineteen years inside of Mag was almost too much for him to control. She peeled his shirt off, letting her fingers across the ripples of his muscles. They unbuckled his shorts together in a frenzy as Mag kicked out of his shoes. His boxers were the last thing she pulled off. She froze in astonishment. The python was at full attention and hungry. She looked up at Mag, a hint of fear in her eyes. "I won't hurt you, I promise."

Mag lifted her onto the four post bed and in one single motion climbed up after her and just admired her body for all those who couldn't. Beauty, freedom, passion; a tear fell from his left eye as he looked into hers. Water flowed onto the bed from hers too. In that moment he realized what had really been taken from him and he was so humbled to have it back. Her high yellow skin was angelic in the moonlight. Her breasts were young and perky, crying to be sucked. Mag fulfilled their wish and continued to explore her every crevice with his tongue all the way down to her honey-pot. Mag allowed his tongue to swim in the vast ocean of her sweetness. Her legs shook. She couldn't be speaking English. Her body must have taken a hint from her legs because it began to convulse and shake too. Mag began to make love to her long and slow. Her eyes rolled, pleasure and pain etched on her face. She was speaking things Mag couldn't understand.

"You feel so good baby, so damn good." Mag said. Her moans sent chills through his body. The pace of their love making grew faster and faster and then it happened for them at the same time.

For a moment they were one with the universe. They totally forgot who they were, lost in space and time, outside of themselves; but only for a second. They collapsed, breathing hard and smiling.

Mag lay holding her in his arms, kissing her with tears in his eyes. He helped to wipe hers away as he kissed her lightly.

"Wow, that was amazing." She said, her body still trembling.

"Amazing doesn't even scratch the surface," Mag said.

She was rubbing his chest with a question in her eyes.

"What's on your mind?" Mag asked.

"After tonight, I mean, what does the future hold for us? Will I ever see you again?" She asked.

"You make me want to stay in this moment forever baby. I feel so good when I'm with you. My dream is to travel the great state of Texas, settle somewhere, stack some bread, then maybe even travel the world. I have to follow my dream baby. How do you feel about coming with me?"

"When are we leaving?" She asked after a minute.

"In a couple of days. I know its short notice, but who can deny that we are twin flames, meant to be together, reunited for a purpose," Mag said, looking deep into her eyes.

She was quiet, thinking. "If I call you in two days then we'll travel the world together Mag. I agree with you. I feel like you complete me. You are who I've been waiting for. If I don't call then even though you're the one it's just not the right timing for me, ok?"

"I can't do nothing but respect that baby." Mag said.

They smiled into each other's eyes. They then celebrated their decision by making love three more times before passing out from exhaustion.

CHAPTER 13: RENEWING THE MIND

The next morning Mag pulled into Jasmine's garage feeling one thousand. His thoughts on the freedom he felt while looking in her eyes, the taste of her lips, her jumping on his back as he walked to the car, hugging her and looking into her captivating soul through her eyes, not knowing if he'd ever see her again.

"Keep your phone by you," she'd said.

"Girl, it would take Armageddon for me not to." Mag remembered saying.

She'd said, "Scott Peck once defined love as: The will to extend one's self for the purpose of nurturing another's spiritual growth. Mag, I can say I love you for it's my wish to extend my heart and mind in whatever way that will foster growth in the spirit of us becoming one."

He'd said, "Yes, and Peck also said that love is too spiritual, too life changing, too eternal to ever be measured or truly understood through words. In the word of God it says that Love is patient, love is kind, it's not self seeking, and that's exactly how I am when I'm with you baby. So from the deepest part of my soul I can say that I love you too."

Mag remembered kissing her before he pulled off. He licked his lips. The faint taste of her still lingered.

Mag noticed that Jasmine's BMW was still warm as his hand slid across the hood. He walked into the house and looked around. 'Surrounded by all this splendor,' Mag thought, 'and this house feels so empty.' The contrast of Stacy's modest home was night and day when it came to how it moved Mag. 'Why am I here?' The thought flickered through his mind.

"Hello, Jazzy, you home?" Mag said.

He heard a door from upstairs open and then close. He looked up. It was Jasmine staring down at him with mixed emotions in her eyes. Her hair was wild, eyes puffy, and she was coming down the stairs fast. She leaped off the bottom step and sprinted in his direction. She jumped up on Mag and wrapped her legs around him and held on for dear life.

"Oh my God Mag," she cried, "I thought I had lost you forever. The phone cut off. I called and texted. Are you okay? What happened? Where did you stay? Who is your friend?"

Mag patted her back as she cried, her body heaving.

Mag said, "Calm down, calm down. I'm good, see? Look." She jumped down from Mag as he turned in circles.

"See, I'm okay. I'm good. I spent the night with a close friend. I'm good." Mag said.

"Mag, I couldn't sleep last night. I was so worried I drove around all morning looking for you. I must have called and texted you fifty times this morning. Why didn't you answer?"

"I never heard the phone ring, not one time. It just kept vibrating and vibrating all morning. I didn't know what the hell was wrong with it."

Mag lied because he knew that the truth would shatter her already damaged heart. He hated to lie, even white ones.

"Oh my God, I'm so stupid. The phones on vibrate. I should have showed you how to work the damn thing, duh," she hit herself in the head flat handed. Guilt threw a left hook and connected to Mag's heart. He didn't know if he was helping her life now or making things worse.

"It's okay. You didn't do anything wrong. Are you ready for our big day riding horses together?" It was his best attempt to change the subject.

"Oh yeah, I almost forgot about that. Look at me. I'm a mess."

"Look," Mag said, "Let's both go and bathe and freshen up and I'll meet you out back in about an hour How does that sound?"

She hugged him sniffling. "Ok, I'm just so happy that you're alright." She tried to hiss him on the mouth. He turned his head and the kiss landed on his cheek instead. Mag walked off. He didn't want to do anything that would lead her on in any way. His plan was to attempt to help her heal before he left. His life coaching grade thus car was a solid C. He had two days left to improve. His grade would only get worse.

Twenty minutes later Mag was soaking in a tub full of bubbles thinking. He understood that it was impossible to understand someone without making room for that person inside of yourself. He knew he would have to have a deep conversation with her soon, but how to approach the subject of her healing without making her angry was the issue he had to work out. He remembered from the book 'The Road Less Traveled' that in any conversation you had to speak on a level the listener can understand and on a level that the listener is mentally and emotionally ready for. He knew that to confront or to criticize another person is a form of exercising leadership or power that shouldn't be taken lightly. How would he reject her desire for more with him and offer her the friendship of healing, offer her an ear that she would have forever? Mag knew that some people would kill for what they wanted. Date Line episodes were filled with stores of rejection gone wrong. He had to be wise with Jasmine.

Mag turned the massage on to help him relax his mind. He had to get this right. Her peace of mind depended on it. He knew from study that there were many ways to help a person escape mental and emotional prisons that they have found themselves trapped in: you could lead by example, use reward and punishment, suggestion, or even what Jesus used, parables.

'What is the right method for this woman, Mag, think.' Something about her story jumped out at Mag and he instantly knew the answer. He remembered that her abductors had brought her back to her dad. She was in a fog and when she heard her dad's voice she had run to him and held on. Mag realized that the same little girl had been holding on ever since, refusing to let go of anything that represented security at all cost.

Mag remembered reading somewhere that when a person cannot direct their own life or determine the quality of their existence then they have something more than just dependent needs and feelings, but they have what psychologists call PDPD, passive dependent personality disorder. They are so hungry looking to be loved that they have no love left over to give back. If love was food on a plate, they'd eat and not get full and couldn't share even if they wanted to. They don't feel love within themselves. They don't feel whole. They always feel like pieces of the puzzle are missing and so they have no real identity. They define themselves by their relationships, but because they have no love to feed their partners, their other half is always scrounging around in other places looking to be fed.

Mag could clearly see now that Jasmine was in a grown woman's body being controlled or influenced by a fearful little girl who can't let go and face the fears that will in turn set her free.

"I'll tell her a parable," Mag said as he turned off the soothing massage stream, "I'll tell her a story and then show her how it connects to her life."

Mag touched the icon that controlled the TV and flipped through the channels on the flat screen. He froze on the news.

Mag didn't want to believe what he thought he'd just seen. He'd caught a glimpse of a Caucasian woman whose face struck him as familiar; he never forgot a face. Names were a different story but a face, he was spot on. Mag turned the TV up and prepared to listen to the reporter standing in front of an apartment building surrounded by crime scene tape. Mag listened.

"I'm Sara Parker and I'm live on the scene of a horrific crime scene. The family of the deceased and police have released the name of the deceased. Lora Smith was stabbed to death in a horrific murder in where the perpetrator removed her fingers and toes before leaving the scene of the crime. Police are saying that rigor mortis shows that her body has been there a day or two at most. Witnesses say they saw a black truck around the area a few days ago that was unfamiliar. If you have any information please call your local police station. The family is asking for prayers and privacy in their time of grief. Back to you Steve."

The thud in Mag's chest woke up, sounding a silent alarm. Mag turned the TV off and walked into the bedroom thinking.

'Lora, Lora, where do I know that name from.' He was pacing the room; names, places, faces, flashing through his minds eyes. Then it hit him from a deep place at the back of his subconscious. The girl from the restaurant on Commerce, Shilo's, could that be her? If it was her would they be suspects? Jasmine had assaulted her. Now she's dead. Who would be crazy enough to cut someone's fingers and toes off? Then the inevitable question screamed in his head, 'Could Jasmine be capable of some shit like this?' Something from within him said no. Then he remembered Jasmine bursting into the room with the keys that morning. Where had she really been that morning? Where else had she went? His dream, the knife, her stabbing him; was it all some kind of sign?

"Think Mag, think, think," he told himself out loud. Maybe I'm just tripping. 'There's a million Lora's in San Antonio. I'm overanalyzing. Plus, I'm leaving in a couple of days anyway after I get my ride.' The fact of her face and his ability to remember faces tried to escape through the surface of his avoiding but his focus was too strong. He paced and rubbed his hands together in anticipation of his dream car arriving. Something whispered to him within as he walked out of the bedroom, 'the lies we tell ourselves are the easiest to tell.'

He met Jasmine out back and she was dressed like a real country cowgirl. The solid black cowboy hat and boots to match took his mind off of the thoughts fighting for attention in his mind. He chuckled.

"What you smiling at papi?" She asked in that heavenly accent. Mag wondered how beauty and pain could be contained so vividly in the same vessel.

"You look like you were born to ride horses. I mean, you got the spurs on and everything." Mag said, looking into her eyes and studying her body language. He'd spent nineteen years around real career killers, men who'd kill their own mothers. He knew the cold detached look they carried in their eyes. Stress and fear had killed their glow, but Jasmine's eyes were not cold. 'It just can't be,' Mag thought, 'I'd be able to feel it. It's my gift.'

The horses that stood before them were majestic. Their muscular frames were impressive, their eyes bold and courageous, ready for war or peace. One was solid black and the other white.

"This big black sexy stallion is King, and his girl the solid white one is Queen." She explained.

Mag loved animals, especially horses. An internal battle plagued him on whether they should be free to roam or used for our benefit. Since God gave us dominion as long as we earned their trust Mag had peace with riding. Mag was stroking Queen's nose and looking into her eyes. He wondered what she was thinking as she looked back at him; from within he let her feel his energy of peace and control, confidence.

"My names Magnum, it's nice to meet you Queen. I'm going to be riding you today. I'll treat you with respect and I'm hoping to get the same in return, ok?" Queen's head rose and fell as if she understood. Mag and Jasmine both chuckled at this.

"I think she has a crush on you Mag. You do know how to ride, don't you?" Jasmine asked.

Mag remembered times at his granddad's ranch, the place where he fell in love with animals and where he learned how to outride most grown men. He was breaking horses by the age of ten. His granddad would say, "You not breaking him son, you earning his respect."

He said, "Jasmine, you just lead the way," and winked. Queen stirred under his weight and then adjusted. "I got you girl, we're good."

The house sat on seven acres of plush country land that included open plains, trails, and wooded areas. You could ride for hours and never get bored.

Jasmine took off on King like a bullet out of a gun, challenging Mag to a race, "Catch me if you can sucker!" Mag was right behind her. The cool morning air felt good on his face. It was all coming back so fast. It took a minute for Mag to get a solid rhythm going but when he connected with the flow of Queen they moved as one.

Mag was right beside Jasmine now. She was looking into his eyes and biting her bottom lip. She seemed to be grinding her hips into the saddle, her hips moving to the rhythm of King's stride. She was leaning forward and rocking back and forth, back and forth.

They were locked in eye contact when her eyes began to roll and her body began to shudder. Her legs were out of the saddle straps hugging King's sides tightly.

She immediately slowed and King began to trot. Mag slowed beside her.

"Did you just?" Mag asked. She blushed, red in the face. No more needed to be said.

They entered a clearing in the woods where the trees seemed to form a circle around them. Netting outlined the circle and a covering over the top allowed fresh sunlight to fill the enclosure. Egyptian styled pillows filled the area.

"Surprise," Jasmine said as they tied the horses just outside of the sitting area. "Please take your shoes off before stepping inside."

The carpet inside the area was plush and soft under Mag's feet. The burgundy and gold color theme of the tent was well styled. A multitude of enormous pillows adorned the sitting area, fluffy and full. A small glass table sat in the middle of the pillows. Atop the table sat a large brown basket and champagne. From somewhere hidden a soft classical music filled the area and put them in a relaxed state as they settled in. Jasmine leaned back on the pillows exposing the wet spot between her legs for just a glimpse. She winked at Mag as he also carved himself out a comfortable niche. She filled the flute glasses to the rim with champagne.

"Wow, you're just full of surprises," Mag said, hinting at the wet spot she'd showed him. The statement had a double meaning.

She blushed again, "Your eyes, I just don't know, I couldn't help myself."

"Get your mind out of the gutter, girl. I'm talking about this magical place in the woods you have here. It's amazing."

Jasmine smirked, "This is my clubhouse, my place of Zen. It relaxes me. On cool nights I sometimes sleep out here with nothing on."

"You're not afraid a bear might come in late at night and steal your honey pot?" Mag asked.

"My honey pot hasn't been stolen in quite some time. No bears around this way, only the occasional deer. My dad hunts and kills them."

Mag felt the moment right for the talk. He had so much to say to try and help but didn't know where to start.

Mag let the champagne set in as they talked about life, politics, and future dreams and goals. Mag realized that she was very smart and sharp minded; her emotional prison was like a cancer in a great body. Mag would try to allow his words to be her radiation treatment.

There was an eerie silence before he began.

"Jasmine, you are beautiful and beloved, a woman of true value. Unique beyond measure and it's truly been a blessing to cross paths with you."

Jasmine blushed and pulled her hair behind her ears, "Thank you, but I, I don't know."

Mag saw the struggle she was having with her spirit within. She was used to seeing herself dirty and unlovable. She wanted to believe Mag's words but they were so foreign.

"Let me finish, let me finish," Mag said as he pulled a pillow into his lap. "Lay down. The story I want to share with you is a true and powerful one that I know of personally. Maybe you will relate. I need you to be fully relaxed and listening with your soul."

Jasmine finished off a grape from the fruit basket and layed her head on the pillow. "Oooh, stories! I love stories."

"Just close your eyes and take long slow breaths, alright?"

Mag waited until he felt her body relax. He was stroking her hair to help her along. He said, "Once upon a time, born into this world was a beautiful baby girl by the name of Maggie. Healthy and strong with a smile that could light up the moon, Maggie hit the ground running. Her mom and dad had to childproof everything because she was adventurous and just wanted to learn. She was full of bubbly joy and her parents were almost concerned that she didn't cry as much as normal little girls."

"When Maggie was seven years old, a friend of the family was entrusted to watch Maggie. In the name of discipline he claimed, while others claimed that a spirit in his didn't agree with Maggie's, he beat Maggie with a belt continuously for an hour straight. No one knows what else he did but after that Maggie was never the same."

Mag noticed that Jasmine's body tensed but he had to make her see his point and so he continued.

"Maggie's spirit was shattered and scarred. She now lashed out at her classmates at school, hitting and biting them. She screamed throughout the night from violent nightmares. Her parents tried everything. Only one person seemed to be able to reach her, her aunt Phillis. Her parents decided it was best that she lived with her aunt and so she moved in with them when she was nine years old. By the time she was eleven, her aunt had taught her that the dark period she had faced and survived was not a reflection of her, but of the person who hurt her. She also taught her that her pain had a purpose and her aunt began to take her to shelters to see other little girls who had been through trauma like her. Soon, Maggie's spirit was back and on fire! She made up her mind that she would use her pain like a farmer uses dung, as fertilizer! Her favorite quote became, 'Either define the moment or the moment will define you,' by Walt Whitman. She chose to define herself as a victor and not a victim. She finally understood that what happened to her wasn't what was going to happen through her! She would be a healer."

Mag noticed that Jasmine had tears in her eyes running wind sprints down her face. He continued, "Jasmine, this girl is my sister. I lost contact with her while I was in prison, but I have no doubt in my mind that she is still fighting to set other girls free from the fear that ensnares them in self imposed prisons."

Jasmine was looking up at the ceiling with tears streaming, a look of hope mixed with fear and apprehension.

"Jasmine, we started this conversation acknowledging how special you are, how smart a woman you are, the dreams that you still carry. This was all stolen from you and it's time you determine to take back your power! For you to define the moment and determine its meaning, a meaning that will empower you and not enslave."

"Jasmine, how long will you allow that beautiful little girl in you to continue to suffer in fear? It's time for you to forgive those men and stop holding so tight to what you think is love but what really is fear."

Jasmine's eyebrows furrowed and she was shaking her head no. Mag kept trying to break through to her inner self. "I understand Jasmine that forgiveness, healing, and fighting for your peace, these new actions involve a risk more powerful and personal and therefore can be more frightening and fearsome than any soldier in a war. A soldier cannot run because when he turns the bullet will hit him in the back of his head. A person taking new action to take their power back can easily retreat back to the detrimental emotions and thoughts they feel have protected them in the past. You can renew your mind, your perspective and grow, forgive, and teach others how to have victory over pain."

Jasmine was still shaking her head no, and now she was saying, "All that bullshit is for the birds: growth, forgive, heal, teach. . . I'm good Mag. What exactly is wrong with me anyway? Those men did what they did. We moved and look at my life. It is what it is. I'm good." She said.

"Jasmine, the moment you held onto your Father, you never let go of him or anything else that represents security. You have become dependent on external things in order to feel loved and worthy when you are already enough!" Mag said.

"I don't know Mag, if I can just find a man to love me through it all maybe I could do the work. Love, true love would help me to feel that way. I'm so alone all the time, even when I'm around people."

"Allowing yourself to depend on another person is the worst thing you could ever do to yourself. It would be better for you to be addicted to coke than for you to depend on a man for fulfillment. As long as you have your fix it'll never let you down. But men will always find a way to disappoint you. Jasmine, it's time for you to start cultivating your own strengths, your independence and individuality, by realizing you have an emptiness and a hunger from trauma that only genuine love for yourself through

God can fill. You have to admit that your emptiness is driving you to initiate and cling to relationships that are harmful to you. Most importantly is understanding that your higher power loves you and has a purpose for your life despite what happened to you."

Jasmine sat up from Mag's lap, "See, I have to do all that just to feel whole, loved, and at peace. You're here and I'm good. I don't want to hear no more, Mag, no more. You hear me? Please!" She was squeezing her fist, her hands turning a light shade of red.

"Alright, alright," Mag said, fighting himself not to address the part 'you're here and I'm good'. "I have to piss anyway. Where is the restroom?"

Jasmine regained her composure. She straightened her hair and dried tears from her eyes with the back of her hands. She said, "I didn't think to have one installed when this place was built. I have a company building me a luxury port-a-potty but until it gets here the nearest tree will have to do," she shrugged her shoulders.

As he walked off she said, "You always trying to heal somebody mind. Damn, heal a bitch body sometimes."

Mag chuckled as he shook the cobwebs from his mind from focusing so intently. In his heart he was losing hope for Jasmine. He understood that growth and healing were the cumulative result of great pain and great disappointment intersecting in a man or woman with a teachable spirit. Jasmine didn't seem to possess a teachable spirit.

As Mag exited the tent the late afternoon air made him breath in deep and relax; freedom. A quick fleeting spark shot through his chest as Stacy's face flashed through his mind. He smiled. He knew that she had just thought about him.

Mag still had an unsettled feeling about what he'd seen on the news earlier but was trying not to think about it. He was standing under a massive pecan tree relieving himself, hoping that the seeds that he'd just planted into Jasmine's soul would take root one day and grow. Mag zipped up and bent down to pick up a shiny object when bark from the pecan tree exploded all around him. He fell to the ground and scrambled away in confusion. Wood chips were in his hair and all over his shoulders. He sholved the object in this pocket

"What the hell!" he said, looking around for some explanation.

Mag stood and walked towards the tree and noticed a rifle slug embedded into the tree, maybe a 30.06 slug. Jasmine was coming out of the tent as Mag heard horse hooves approaching from the north.

Victor rode up to where they stood with a large rifle in his right hand. He said, "Did you see a deer run through here?" He was glaring at Mag.

"Do I look like a fucking deer old man? You almost shot me in my damn head. What the hell is wrong with you? Are you crazy?" Mag asked while knocking wood chips from his head and shoulders.

"Wind must have carried the bullet. Happens sometimes." Victor's tone was casual and low as if almost taking Mag's life was nothing.

"Happens sometimes!" Mag lunged towards Victor but Jasmine stepped in the way.

"No Mag! Please don't. Calm down, please!" Jasmine said.

Mag pointed his finger towards Victor, his eyes fighting red. He couldn't find the words to fit his rage. Victor smirked at Mag, turned his horse around and rode off.

"Calm down, Mag. Please breathe, ok?" Jasmine said.

"I wouldn't be breathing at all if I wouldn't have bent down to pick up something. He's talking about a fuckin deer. I got his deer alright."

"It was an accident Mag. He didn't mean it. You heard him."

"Did you see that big ass scope on his rifle? Accident my ass."

"The wind Mag, it sometimes carries bullets. Why would he want to hurt you? Why Mag?"

"For the next couple of days it would be wise if you kept your pops away from me altogether." Mag said. He walked off and jumped on Queen and rode off towards the main house. Jasmine was right behind him. He tied Queen where he had found her. Jasmine caught up with him in the kitchen.

"I apologize for my dad's actions today Mag. It could have been a lot worse, right?"

"Damn right it could have been worse! He could have blown my damn head off. Then what, huh?"

Tears formed in her eyes. She looked exhausted, as if life wouldn't give her a moment of peace, of rest. "Look Mag, I just want to thank you for your kind words out there. They really meant a lot to me and even though I got kind of upset at the end, your words really touched me. Tomorrow I'm going to talk to some outpatient treatment centers. I'll be gone until about three or four in the afternoon, ok?"

Mag just walked off thinking if it wasn't for him waiting on Stacy's call he'd say forget the car and just leave. He took a quick shower and laid back in the plush bed thinking about Stacy and if he should call her, tell her he was on his way, that he needed to feel the essence of her love near him. He knew leaving with him would be a big decision for her to make and he didn't want her to feel pressured so he decided against calling her. He fell asleep thinking, 'Why am I really still here?'

CHAPTER 14: THE HOOK

SNAP! Mag shot up in bed rubbing his legs. "Damn that felt real," he whispered to himself. He'd just dreamed that he'd stumbled upon a huge pile of money and he just so happened to have a large tan duffle bag with him. He looked to his left and then took a quick glance to his right. Coast clear, an anxious smile crept onto his face as if the smile was its own. Mag had slowly crept up to the pile of hundred dollar bills. He grabbed a handful and stuffed it in the bag. He paused, scanned his surroundings, nil, no one was watching him. He stuffed another handful of hundreds into his bag not believing his fortune. The more money he stuffed into the bag the more excited he got. The more excited he got the faster his hand moved. His excitement blinded him to the lever swinging fast over the top of his head and slamming down hard on his legs, SNAP!

Mag remembered reading that dreams were a form of your subconscious letting free what the conscious mind tries to suppress during the day when awake. These avoided thoughts, now during sleep not having anything to guard them were free to flow.

Mag yawned and wiped sleep from his eyes, 'What was that dream trying to tell me?' Mag thought to himself as he slipped on some jogging pants. 'What am I missing? What is the spirit trying to show me? What is this unrest within my soul?' Mag slipped on some running shoes. It was time for him to take a trip within himself to see what he was hiding from. First the voice about the amount of cheese one gets to eat before the snap, and now the dream about the mouse trap with a pile of money as the cheese. He had to figure it out. It was something important. He had learned the hard way the importance of listening to this voice. In prison he had started seeing images of the Trojan horse in his head at different times throughout the day. At night dreams of him at the hospital getting knives pulled out of his back started to plague his sleep. A week later one of the people in his crew whom he felt he could trust tried to shank him over attention he was getting from a female guard. He escaped the incident with his life and the lesson: Listen to your other self! It will protect you from potential danger.

As Mag brushed his teeth he thought about something his granddad told him while they were out fishing one day, "Grandson, I want you to listen to me and I need you to listen good. You'll never see a man throw a bare hook into the water. The fish would just swim up to the hook, give it a quick glance, and then swim off. But what we do is cover the hook with a fat juicy worm that's just too irresistible for the fish."

Mag remembered listening intently to his grandfather, eager to learn.

"Now look at my bobber out there son, watch it. Did you see it move?"

"Yes sir granddad, I seen it move."

"See son the fish just took his first bite and then backed up to savor the taste. Watch." His granddad had said.

Sure enough a couple minutes later the bobber moved again. Mag remembered jumping to his feet in excitement. "What's he doing now granddaddy?" Young Mag had asked.

"He just took himself an even bigger bite son. And now greed is about to take over cause the worm is just too good to 'em. Now he'll take the whole thing into his mouth and make a run for it which will cost him, watch."

All of a sudden the bobber disappeared from the surface of the water. Mag remembered seeing his granddad stand up and yank back on the fishing pole and began to reel the fish in. His granddad unhooked the fish and threw him back into the water.

"See son I could have taken him home and cooked him but sometimes in life the good Lord gives us another chance. Either he'll become a wise fish and learn to nibble the bait from the hook a little bit at a time or someone else will catch him and he might not be so blessed next time son."

"I would have ate him granddad. I'm hungry." Young Mag had said.

His granddad chuckled, "The moral son is you must always look for the hook in a potential dangerous situation. Never allow greed to blind your wisdom. Always allow knowledge and wisdom to show you the hook, okay?"

"Yes sir," Mag remembered answering.

As he finished brushing his teeth and washing his face he knew somehow he was failing to apply that lesson to his life at the moment. He wondered how much time he had until this situation yanked back on him and reeled him in.

In the kitchen Mag noticed that it was 9:30 in the morning on the microwave. He poured himself a tall glass of orange juice and savored it slowly as the pulp flowed over his tongue, his first glass in nineteen years. As he sat and ate the bacon and eggs he flipped through the channels hoping to catch the news story from the other day to get a better look at the woman's face. No local news was on, and he damn sure wasn't about to watch Fox news.

Mag turned the TV off and finished his breakfast in silence. Outside on the patio Mag went through his stretch routine. The coolness of the morning air was refreshing, all the open space made Mag smile. Not a cell bar in sight, no guards yelling 'chow time', or 'pair it up on the run', or 'rack up', nil, just him and his freedom.

As he ran he remembered to breathe rhythmically in a 2:1 pattern, two strides per breath, because it takes stress off the respiratory muscle and reduces fatigue compared to the 2:2 pattern of breathing, breathing in for two steps and out for two steps. Mag looked down at his wrist and realized that he forgot to wear his watch. He couldn't challenge himself to run an eight minute mile.

Mag passed the large cabin on his right. So attractive, yet so cold and distant, homeless even. A foul stench attacked his nose for a moment and then it was gone, something dead in the distance. The open flat plains ended and Mag entered a wooded area with a trail running through it. Ten minutes later he came up on the area where the trees created a natural clearing. He walked over to the tree where he had taken a piss and rubbed his hand over the bullet hole. "Crazy ass old man," he whispered to the tree, half for his sake and half because he noticed the dried up sap the tree had bled.

Mag entered the area with pillows. The champagne bottle and the fruit basket were still present. Mag took a swig to soothe his lungs from the run. Mag's heart rate had slowed and the cool morning air coming through the netting was drying his sweat.

Something new was gnawing at his conscious, something he'd noticed in the wooded area unconsciously was now attempting to force its way into Mag's conscious. He shook it off. Now was time for looking within.

Mag kicked his shoes off and lay back on the pillow. He slowed his breathing, slowly in through his nose and out slowly through his mouth. 'The cheese is your weakness,' he heard a voice from within say. "Why?" Mag asked his subconscious. It seemed as if his subconscious was trying to do two things at once. Push its own agenda by telling Mag to focus on what he'd saw in the wooded area, and then on the other hand obeying its command to find the answer to his question.

"Why is the cheese your weakness Mag?" He asked himself. "Focus." His soul took him back to a time before his dad sold drugs and hustled to make ends meet. Mag had to be eight or nine years old, early 90's, late 80's, he couldn't remember exactly. It's another morning, another dreaded first day of school. Mag remembered the first day of school at his school being like a fashion show, a day of showing off your new shoes and matching clothes, your backpack and fresh school supplies. This wasn't so for Mag.

Mag was now in a sort of self hypnosis state, fully absorbed in what his subconscious was showing him.

The first day of school was embarrassing for Mag, for his dad was struggling just to keep a roof over their head and food in their stomachs, let alone buy new school clothes, shoes, and supplies. Mag's dad was a strong willed man but some days Mag would walk in and see the strain in his eyes, a man dealing with the strain of failing at his duty to do the basic element of American manhood: provide.

In his mind Mag saw himself walking down the hallway with his hand-me-down, dark purple, Salvation Army issued backpack strapped to his back.

"Look ya'll, he has a girl backpack on. Hey Mag, didn't you have those same shoes on in the fifth grade?"

An explosion of laughter would erupt around him. He remembered them pointing fingers and chanting, "Fag, fag, Mag the fag," all because of his purple backpack which his father said represented the violet flame of protection, yea right.

Mag remembered now feeling so low, so worthless, like a bum, a no body. This went on for a few years until his dad taught him how to fight.

"Son, you never let another man disrespected you. Look at me in my eyes when I'm talking to you, damn it! Next time that sucka talks about your shoes or anything else you bust him in his damn mouth and take his! You bet not never come to me crying again about people picking on you, now put your hands up."

That next year Mag was ten, maybe eleven. Instead of going through the front of the school he crept through the side and waited at a vantage point where he could see the bully go in the restroom. Mag slid in behind the bully in the restroom and locked the door behind him.

"Well look who we have here, if it isn't Mag the fag," the bully said.

Mag was dead locked onto the bully's eyes with focus and determination like his dad had taught him. He'd said it was something about direct eye contact that made a man nervous. Mag cracked his knuckles for affect. He noticed a hint of fear in the bully's eyes now that he didn't have a crowd around him.

"What size shoes do you wear?" Mag asked.

"Your size fag, why?"

"That's good for me and bad for you punk." Mag felt possessed. He was fueled by all the years of built up anger and humiliation that he had suppressed; ridicule, rejection, and revenge cheering him on.

"What are you going to do? Huh fag?" The bully asked.

Mag picked up on the quiver in the bully's voice. "I'll tell you exactly what's going to happen," Mag said, "You can take off my Jordans on your feet and my Dallas Cowboy's backpack from your back and get beat up with mercy, or I'm going to bust you up baaaad and take 'em anyway. Your choice."

The bully dropped his backpack and stood in an awkward stance with his fist balled up. Mag noticed his hands slightly shaking. Looking at him Mag didn't even see a person, he saw the poverty that made him feel as if his worth was of external existence, that made him feel as if all he had to offer the world was worthless.

Mag laughed at him, "You don't know how to fight, do you sissy. I think we've found out who the real fag is."

Mag wanted to totally humiliate him so he decided to fight the bully open handed. Mag slapped the bully around the restroom for five whole minutes until he was humiliated, crying, and pleading, "Ok, ok, you can have them Mag!"

Mag now remembered leaving the restroom feeling like a King with the Jordans on and the new backpack. He didn't understand how something external could cover an inner feeling of worthlessness, his young mind not able to put the pieces of the puzzle together.

"Cool man! Are those the new Air Jordans?" Someone asked.

"You know it," Mag said as if Jordans were the only shoes he ever wore.

"Cool backpack Mag," said a girl he knew of but whom had never even spoken a word to him until that moment.

"Thank you," Mag walked away from the girl feeling on top of the world.

'At that moment right there in your mind material things became the way to receive love, recognition, and acceptance,' Mag heard a voice in his soul say. The soft voice within him always sounded like a woman's voice; he wondered if it was his mother's voice guiding him from beyond.

Mag didn't like to think of his mother because then he had to think about what had happened to her, what his father had done to her when he was fourteen, five years before he went to prison. Mag just told everyone who asked that she had died while giving birth to him. The truth was just too hard to handle; his dad shot and killed her! Mag wondered if his dad was alive, still in prison, or out doing good for himself. He lost contact with everyone.

The wooded area flashed into his mind again. In the thicket of the woods he'd noticed something as he had jogged by. He hadn't paid it much attention but his subconscious had. Mag tried to shake the invading thought. It was vital he connect his weakness for cheese to what he had went through growing up and then heal that part of him so that he wouldn't get trapped in this cycle over and over. Mag knew he had to update the outdated map of his mind if he was going to have clearer direction for the future. His subconscious wouldn't let it go and he could no longer focus. 'Ok, I'll go check it out,' he told himself.

Mag came-to from his hypnosis state and realized that he was extremely thirsty. He took another swig of the now stale champagne just to wet his throat. He stood, shook his muscles loose, and took off jogging towards the wooded area.

When Mag entered the wooded area by the trail he slowed to a walk. On the way he was relying on his spirit to lead him back to the exact spot. On the way in something on his right hand side of the trail had caught his attention; he now focused his attention on the left.

At about the midpoint of the pathway Mag craned his neck looking deep into the brush and noticed a pile of loose dirt about eight feet long and four feet wide. Clearly it was a shallow grave of some kind and well concealed for some reason. Mag had an urge to make his way through the thicket to get a closer look at the possible grave, heard something move in the brush and decided against it.

Back at the house the microwave showed that it was 12:30. 'Damn, I've been gone three hours. How long did I stay in that trance soul searching?'

Mag fixed himself two sandwiches with the works and a tall glass of apple juice to wash it down. The house was quiet. Mag figured Jasmine wasn't back yet; she'd mentioned coming back later this afternoon. As he ate his mind was busy trying to figure out what it all meant: Jasmine's crazy outbursts, the shadow out-side of Stacy's house that night, him feeling like they were being followed while at the zoo, the girl on the news from the restau-rant, her fingers and toes missing, the shallow grave, a woman's voice deep within his soul with a weird question about cheese, and what did his childhood have to do with his current situation?

'What does it all mean? Am I paranoid and merging things that don't go together like puzzle pieces that don't fit?' One thing he knew for sure, where there was smoke there was either fire or one that had been put out. Maybe the cheese was hindering his judgement? Maybe he was blinded by what he thought was a blessing but was really a test. He had to put it all together before he moved on.

At that moment an idea popped into his head. He decided he'd search the house. There had to be something there that could ex-plain who Jasmine was, who he was dealing with, something that would help shape his perspective. Mag knew that if he was going to do it that he had to do it now before she got back. She could pop up at any moment.

Mag placed the plate and glass into the dishwasher and started right there searching the kitchen. Part of himself felt like a fool, the other part needed to know something, anything to help it make the puzzle fit. Why would her uncle Torrez try to shank him right before he got released, knowing that, why the hell did he get in the car?

He found nothing. No guns in the drawers, no money stashed in a tin can labeled flour, no hollow kitchen floor like in the mov-ie 'Training Day'.

The living room might as well have been a show piece at Rent-a-center. The plastic was still on the furniture, the glass table was spotless, and the picture on the wall looked as if someone used a level to get them straight, nothing crazy under the sofas.

The house had a still calm, the type that comes before a raging storm. It was soundless except for the noise Mag was making.

The guest bedrooms on the second floor might as well have come from 'Rooms to Go'. They were elegantly decorated, strong oak four post beds, huge flat screens. Jasmine's husband was definitely a na'bob. Nil was in the rooms. The rooms were void of anything Mag could use to add to the puzzle to make the picture clearer. No safe behind a picture frame with a secret diary saying, 'I killed my husband, the girl at the restaurant, and I have another body buried out back'. He closed the guest bedroom door and stood quiet on the second floor to make sure he heard no cars pulling in. The coast was clear. Mag moved on to where he now wished he would have began in the first place, her bedroom.

CHAPTER 15: THE SEARCH

With still no other sound in the house Mag opened Jasmine's bedroom door and slid in like a Navy Seal on a secret mission. He started at her massive oak dresser with the golden handles; the design was bold but feminine. The surface of the dresser had a woman's normal accessories: make-up, perfumes, and curling irons. In the drawers is where panties, nighties, socks, and undershirts were kept. Mag felt somewhat like a peeping tom, but knew motive is what made all the difference. Under her panties Mag found a sex toy that resembled a rose of some sort. Mag guessed that it was meant to directly stimulate a woman's most sensitive spot, getting the job done quick, fast, and in a hurry.

Mag rearranged the contents of the drawer and closed it, nil. Mag found the remote to the bed and lowered it to the ground. Most people kept something underneath their bed. It was like a hen sleeping on a nest egg, it just felt safer there. Mag lifted the mattress and instantly noticed the two pearl handled twenty fives. They were small and compact with one of the most dangerous bullets in the world because it bounces around the body off bones. Mag let the mattress down and checked the clips, fully loaded. He smelled the weapons. They hadn't been fired recently. Other than some K-Y jelly and a small sized pink vibrator, nothing else was under the bed. Mag let the bed back down and put the remote into his pocket.

Mag checked her nightstand clock and saw that it was 1:25 PM. He'd been searching the house for almost an hour now fueled by the feeling that he was getting close to something that would clear the puzzle. He was almost finished. Just one more spot to check: her closet.

From the outside her closet looked smaller than what it really was but once inside Mag was surprised to find that it was the size of a small children's bedroom, two times bigger than the cell Mag had just spent the last nineteen years in. Straight ahead, up against the back wall facing Mag was a sturdy looking safe, the kind with the high school combination lock. On the right hand side of the closet Mag saw hundreds of elegant dresses of all colors. The light in the closet must have been activated by motion detection for it to came on as soon as Mag stepped in.

The left side of the closet was adorned with warm looking winter coats made from different animals. Mag also noticed lace shirts and other women's tops that were unmistakably high end. Further inside the closet closer to the safe on both sides were hundreds of tasteful women's heels of all sorts. Mag checked the safe handle. It was locked.

The top shelves on both sides were full of boxes and packages. Photo albums sat stacked against one another in order of year. 'If I were trying to hide something where would I put it?' Mag thought. Most right handed people kept important things on the right by nature. Since Jasmine was left handed Mag focused on her natural side of the closet.

In the corner on the left hand side of the shelf Mag noticed a dark black box with a stack of books on top trying to conceal it.

Mag unstacked the books and removed the box. He sat up under the light on a set of small steps meant to help Jasmine reach the top.

Inside the box on top Mag noticed old newspaper clippings. 'Three Men Found Mutilated.' Mag read the clipping and realized it was from Mexico. Three men had been tortured so bad that it was hard for police to identify them as human at first. What stood out to Mag was that the victims had their tongues cut out and they were missing their fingers and toes. "Why would she keep this clipping?" Mag whispered to himself. An eerie feeling started to creep in and settle itself within Mag's spirit. Mag found another clipping with the heading: 'Multi-Millionaire Disappears'. The article detailed suspicion that foul play was involved mostly motivated by money. The wife, Jasmine Cruz, having the most to gain. Mag found next to the article a legal document saying that Jasmine's net worth was one hundred and forty five million dollars, not including the awaited insurance check that was being processed.

The next thing that Mag found left him bemused, "What the hell?" Mag shifted towards the light to get a better look, his mind not really understanding what he was looking at or just in plain disbelief. It was a printout of his personal profile from a website called Write-A-Prisoner.

On the paper Jasmine had made notes and circled things Mag guessed she felt were important. Blood had rushed to his head, the beat-drum had picked up again, his mind straining to put things together; this is what he was looking for.

Mag noticed that his prison discharge date was circled over and over and over again like it was some point of emphasis. Next to his picture was scribbled a note: 'Santa Muerte says this man will be mine one day.' The page looked like it was stained with a few drops of blood, "What the fuck. . ." Mag didn't even hear himself say the words. 'She had this shit all planned out the whole time,' Mag thought to himself, 'How could I not have seen it?' Mag thought back to the day in the parking lot, her uncle Torrez '. . . but that story was real. . . if she wanted me as hers why did her uncle try and kill me? How did she line up his release date with mine?'

If Mag had any kind of psychological disorder it certainly wasn't a character disorder in where the person looked for fault outside of himself for blame. If anything he was more neurotic in the sense that he took too much of the blame as if it was all his fault. His grandpa had taught him to always be aware, and when something got past him he was hard on himself.

In chess a master player is known to calculate up to three to four moves ahead. Mag had only been focused on two moves: giving Jasmine tools to heal and getting his car and leaving. 'The cheese is your weakness,' he heard the voice again. 'Yeah, you right. I should have been gone,' he thought.

Mag sat thinking, gripping the printout of his profile in his hands thinking about his next move knowing what he knew. He heard distant footsteps coming up the steps. "Shit!"

Mag stuffed the papers back into the box and slammed the lid on throwing the box back in place and replacing the books as close to their original state as possible. By the time he had everything put in place he heard her voice on the third floor. 'Damn, think fast Mag, think fast.' His adrenaline was moving fast through his body and sweat had started to show up for the party on his forehead.

Mag thought, 'I could burst out of the closet with the profile and confront her with what I had just found. No, that would reveal my cards and could get ugly fast. Not yet.'

"Mag, are you in there?" Her voice sounded muffled as if she was standing at his bedroom door. Mag heard Jasmine walk into the bedroom where he was and throw a set of keys down on the nightstand. Mag had no visual from the closet like in most movies. It didn't work out quite like that in real life. 'Think quick Mag, think.' Mag felt the remote to Jasmine's bed still in his pocket and an idea came to his mind.

Mag burst out of the closet. Jasmine jumped back startled. Mag pushed the button on the remote for music and slow Jazz music filled the room. Mag had been strip searched so much in prison by guards that he was practically a professional stripper. He started moving his body in a seductive manner. Jasmine's face instantly turned from one of shock to intrigue. Mag noticed a bottle of baby oil on her dresser and applied some in a smooth manner into his hand and rubbed it all over his chest and abs. He was already shirtless from his morning run.

Mag pushed the button for the bed and it descended to the ground level. He made a hand motion directing her to take a seat. She slid on to the bed biting her bottom lip as he moved his body. Mag noticed that she'd hiked up her skirt and had begun to touch herself in a sensual manner.

Mag said, "You've been wanting me since the first day you laid eyes on me right mami?"

"Oh yes, papi, so bad, so bad." She said.

She continued to touch herself as Mag continued to move his body, giving her sneak peeks of the python little glimpses at a time. Mag could hear audible moans coming from Jasmine. She was close, her mind a thousand miles away from the fact that he was just in her closet. Her body began to heave and tremble, one hand gripping the sheet, her eyes rolling before she went limp. Mag stopped dancing.

He said, "Meet me in a couple of hours on the second floor in the theater room and we'll chop it up. That surprise was for the effort you took today to seek healing. I'm proud of you. If you're good later I might even consider letting the python out to play."

"Yes sir," Jasmine said.

Mag walked to his room thinking for no particular reason that the word python was from the name of a large dragon guarding the chasm at Delphi. It was killed by Apollo who established his temple there. His python was very much still alive. If she wanted to game, then game on.

❖　❖　❖

Jasmine and Mag sat in the kitchen and ate a homemade meal of flour tortillas, fajita meat, beans and rice, and a side of mild salsa. They would lock eyes in between bites, their eyes saying different things. Mag's was saying, 'so you wanna play', while her eyes showed sexual anticipation motivated by the show Mag had given her earlier. They said, 'I've been waiting on this moment for years.'

As the sun descended for its nap they retired to the second floor theater room feeling full, relaxed, and a little tipsy from the Grey Goose on the rocks they had been sipping. As she surfed through the channels searching for a move, Mag was being plagued by pride and an unwillingness to accept that he had been played, tricked, deceived. He was doing his best to shake the emotions.

Jasmine chose a movie called 'Sleepers' about some young boys who were beaten and molested in a boys home and then grew up to repay each guard one by one. The movie was a classic in Mag's eyes but at the moment his body language showed indifference.

After the movie was over Jasmine excused herself, "I'll be right back. Don't move." she said. When she was upstairs and out of sight Mag paced the room and thought, 'She think that I'm stuck in her web but she got another thing coming. I had compassion on her issues and she tried to play me like a fool. I got something for her.' A quote that Mag had learned while in prison came to his mind, 'Be a pianist, not a piano.' He nodded his head in agreement with his inner self.

Proverbs 20:9 popped into his mind for some reason as he paced the room, 'BEFORE DESTRUCTION THE HEART OF THE MAN IS PROUD'. The voice seemed aggressive and assertive. Mag ignored the voice knowing that those whom choose to lie, manipulate, and betray those who care for you unleash the law of perfect justice to receive the same in return. The scales always balance out. It never fails.

A small feeling at the back of his mind was hoping that something would save him from himself, from what he might do in this mindset. He checked his phone hoping against hope that he'd missed a call from Stacy saying that she'd be ready to leave in the morning and to be there early or to come over tonight. Nil, no missed calls. He wondered would a text be invading her space, or was not texting or calling coming off like 'I got what I wanted'. He had been out of the dating game for so long. He shook the doubts and trusted the connection that they had. He made a quick decision: if the car was ready in the morning then he'd pack his shit and just go by. He couldn't wait any longer. IF she wasn't ready to leave he would leave and just give her time. This situation was getting way out of hand.

Jasmine came down the stairs in an all black see-through nighty with fur around the bottom. Mag could see the anticipation in her eyes. Her body was tight and firm underneath the lace. She turned the TV to an R&B station and Avant 'When We Make Love' filled the room. 'I got yo legs spread all over the bed, hands clinging to the sheets, hair wild as hell I know, the only thing on ya mind is sexing me girl. . .'

Jasmine said, "I thought I'd return the favor." She began to move her body to the melody of the music. Mag sat back thinking about his options. He could get her mind riled up to the point of exploding then leave her yearning, or you could 'beat her back in' and express his mental frustration physically. Pride and Grey Goose made the decision for him.

Mag motioned with his finger for her to 'come here'. She stopped dancing and obeyed. He bent her over and entered her from behind. She must have been warmed up and already ready to go because there was no kissing her body, no looking deep into her eyes, nil, just straight 'pound game'. Ten minutes later he exploded. She did for the second time and he walked straight to his room. No cuddling, no intimate pillow talk, just a mug on his face.

As Mag walked off she was panting, struggling to get her words out, "Oh my God, that was amazing, powerful, aggressive. Thank you, thank you, I needed that."

Chapter 16: Drive

Mag woke up and hadn't even remembered falling asleep. The nightstand held a clock that said it was July 1st and Mag for some reason remembered that July was the month that Julius Ceaser was born and got his name from and not the other way around like a lot of people thought. Actually, even earlier than that the month of July was called Quintilis, the fifth month. Mag didn't know why little facts like this stayed in his head once he read about them.

Mag was surprised that Jasmine hadn't tried to come into his room for another round during the night. She had been gone all yesterday morning. Maybe she was tired from being dug into mentally and also physically.

Mag stretched out on the bed allowing the vibration of the stretch to reverberate through his body. He spoke a manifestation over his day, "Today is going to be a good day! I'll soak for the last time in that soothing Jacuzzi tub, my old-school Cadi will show up, Stacy is going to call and say she is ready to travel with ya boy, and I'll take whatever lessons from this situation that God has for me."

Mag spoke these words into the atmosphere as he looked up at the ceiling. He had read somewhere that when you speak good things into existence they manifest and come to pass. It had worked for him in the past, but boy would it fail to work for him this day.

Mag looked over at the clock and was surprised that he had slept so late. Maybe he too was tired both mentally and physically. It was already 3:30 PM. He figured the Grey Goose played a part in his exhaustion. He stretched out one last time and hopped out of the bed.

Inside the bathroom he added bubble solution to the tub and started the warm water. As he was brushing his teeth he thought about the fact that he'd already had sex with two women, one out of pleasure and the other frustration. The average American has sex 56.9 times a year. Married couples were at 96.3 times a year the last time Mag read. This averaged out at two times a week. Mag figured he'd be hard pressed to catch the married couples but at the rate he was going the singles were in trouble. He smiled at the thought.

In the bedroom Mag was on his last set of twenty sets of fifty pushups when his cell phone started ringing on the nightstand. He disconnected it from the charger, "Please be my baby, please be Stacy." It wasn't Stacy. Mag didn't recognize the number, "Mag speaking."

"This is Matt Gibson at Auto Pro Alamo. I'm calling for a Mr. Ty Magnum. . ." The man sounded frustrated but professional at the same time as if he had carried some personal issues from home to work.

Excitement flashed through Mag's torso, "Mr. Gibson, Mr. Gibson, man is it good to hear your call," Mag said.

Gibson chuckled, "Well good afternoon Mag, I'm calling to inform you that we have finished the custom paint job on the 1982 El-dog convertible. She came out shining like new money sir. I commend your taste. If you ever get tired of her just call."

"That's my baby. I love her and we haven't even met yet," Mag joked, "we gone be together for life. Sorry Matt."

"Sir, I bet you're anxious to drive her and we'll be delivering her as instructed to you later this afternoon. Is the delivery address the same?"

"Yes sir, same spot," Mag said.

"Well then, I'll see you this afternoon and thank you for doing business with Auto Pro Alamo. Please spread the word."

"I will and the pleasure is mine. Matt, remember this, kites rise highest against the wind, not with it."

Mag hung up, "YES!!!" He was doing a little dance picturing himself rolling down the highway. If this is what getting played felt like then he was all for the games. "I knew it was going to be a good day. I said it. I spoke it." He was pumping his fist to himself. His dream was now a reality.

Mag finished his last set of pushups, rubbed his hands together in anticipation of good things to come, and went to take his last bath as planned. It would be his last.

The water pressure felt so soothing as it eased away the stress of the last few days. Soul searching to find inner answers that have been laying dormant, dealing with the up and down roller coaster emotional state of Jasmine, wondering if Stacy was thinking of him and if she would leave with him, and not to mention almost being shot in the head was nerve racking. In life you had to take the good and the bad, the blessings and the curses, the ups with the downs, in the course of a day one could smile and one could frown; Yin and Yang.

Comfort always came with the thoughts of the open road and of Stacy on his side as they ate up the miles of highway. Everything that he owned was already packed. He decided he'd wear his Rolex and ring that manipulation had paid for, not to mention it had almost cost him his life. He'd leave in style.

Again he looked at his situation as fortune, as favor. Just days ago he was sitting inside of a small prison cell washing his t-shirt and shorts from inside of the toilet. He had been considered by society as the lowest of the lowest and now he was sitting in a three story mansion soaking in a mini swimming pool and waiting for a brand new old school Lac to be dropped off so that he could travel Texas with one of the most beautiful women he had ever seen. He knew thousands of men that would trade places with him this very moment. Yes, he would take the good with the bad. Blessings were sometimes packaged inside of pain.

Mag knew that the facts of our lives are not as important as our attitudes towards those facts. He'd learned that the hard way. And even though he'd spent nineteen years in prison, he always knew that his time would come to shine.

'HOW MUCH CHEESE DOES A MOUSE GET TO EAT BEFORE THE TRAP SNAPS HIM?' The voice within him seemed to scream at him, almost pleading for him to pay attention. Mag shook the thought, 'this ain't no damn trap, it's a blessing.' Wanting to get his mind off the voice he grabbed the iPad remote and flipped through the channels. The 5:00 news was just starting with breaking news. The picture on the screen made Mag stand up in the tub with his mouth wide open!

CHAPTER 17: DEATH

The screen was flashing: Breaking news, Breaking news!!! A hurricane of emotion shot through Mag's body. He almost lost his balance. An unsettling fear began to attack the pit of Mag's stomach snaking its way up towards his head like a lit fuse that would cause a catastrophic explosion once the reality of what he was seeing was realized.

"This is Michelle Kay reporting live from the scene of another horrific crime in the last couple of days. A twenty three year old San Antonio Spurs cheerleader by the name of Stacy Jones was found bludgeoned to death in her home early this morning. Her bags seemed to be packed as if she was about to leave. Police say we may have a serial killer on the loose because Stacy's fingers and toes were removed in the same way as a victim earlier this week. Police are asking people to stay in groups. Stacy's time of death is stated as somewhere in the early morning hours yesterday. If you have any information please call the police. I'm Michelle Kay reporting back to you Steve."

Mag fell and then stood back up, his fist unconsciously clinched, a stream of tears cascading from his eyes and creating rivers on his cheeks. The inside of his chest was on fire, his thoughts jumbled, grief and anger possessing him like an evil spirit; the fuse reached his head and exploded.

"Jasmine!" Mag yelled with all the rage he could muster. She has claimed to be gone all day yesterday seeing some specialist. Mag now knew exactly what she had been doing. First Lora and now Stacy, the trap had finally snapped.

He leaped out of the tub in a blinding rage flinging water everywhere and rushed into the room to get dressed as the puzzle unfolded in his mind. Fingers and toes cut off, same M.O. in both Lora's and my baby's murder. In both murders she was gone at their estimated time of death. Fingers and toes inside the bucket in the room where the kidnappers held her. She looked inside and that evil snuck into her. The newspaper clippings in her closet, the three guys mutilated in Mexico, fingers and toes missing. It all made sense.

Mag lost control and hit the bedroom floor as pain ravaged his body, tears and snot flowed as he tried to pull himself together. To think about her last moments, her bags packed. . . Now dressed, Mag threw open the door, "Jasmine!" he yelled, tears still running down his face, his mind not feeding off blood but vengeance.

Stacy's face flashed in his mind as he kicked open Jasmine's bedroom door, wood splinters exploding from the hinges. Her room was empty.

An image of Stacy's body flashed through Mag's mind, how it glistened in the moonlight, the passion in her eyes as he stroked her. That passion now would forever be a memory.

"Jasmine, I know, you evil conniving tramp. Where are you?"

Mag thought about him and Stacy at the zoo, the natural way they vibed together, the way they seemed to be made for one another. Mag checked the guest bedrooms, nil. "WHY, HUH?"

The pain was evident in Mag's voice. "Why'd you have to kill her? I saw your shadow outside her house that night. Why not take my life? Do you hear me you crazy stalking bitch!"

Mag kicked a massive hole in the plasma flat screen and then descended the stairs. He checked the garage. Both cars were there. "Where are you?" Mag yelled as he kicked over the glass table in the living room.

A picture of Stacy flashed through his mind of her jumping on his back that last day. He remembered piggybacking her to the car. She was giggling the whole time, her smile radiant in the morning sun. It felt like someone had poured acid on his heart, it burned so bad. The kitchen was empty. Mag opened the sliding glass door and stood on the patio, "Jasmine, where are you slut? You think that old man out there can save you from this ass wh-upping?" Mag was locked on the cabin in the distance.

The evening air was cool but hot to Mag. He was a volcano ready to burn with his lava. The phone vibrated in Mag's pocket.

"Stacy tell me I'm in a nightmare baby and this is you!"

"Uhhh, this is Matt Gibson calling to tell you that your car is parked in your driveway. We left the keys in between the driver side sun visor after no one answered our knock." "Yeah, ok." Mag hung up.

In the distance Mag noticed a faint light coming from the cabin.

"Got your ass now!" Mag took off jogging towards the cabin, retaliation his number one goal in life.

Mag came up on the side of the cabin slightly out of breath from the run and some due to the adrenaline coursing through his body. He paused under the window to catch his breath. The sun was starting to get sleepy. It already had its pajama's on and was brushing its teeth for the night.

He stood and looked in the window. It was a kitchen and it was empty. Mag crept around to the back of the cabin and checked the back door. It was locked. Sitting under a strongly built wooden shed was a solid black GMC truck. Mag remembered the news saying that the witness saw a black truck driving around Lora's apartment and from somewhere deep in his subconscious Mag remembered seeing a black truck driving off when he'd stepped onto Stacy's porch.

'She thought she was slick driving her father's truck, but I see all the pieces now,' Mag thought.

He wanted to keep the element of surprise just in case her father was there and he had to deal with them both. It took everything in his power to suppress his screams of rage. The sun had finally closed its eyes and provided a good cover as he crept around to the front of the cabin. He stooped beside the steps. The night was quiet, his heart loud.

There was a peculiar stench in the air around the cabin. Maybe something had died far off in the wood and the odor was riding the waves of the wind or maybe Victor had a deer cleaning station close by. Something was definitely violating his sense of smell.

'This has to be a dream. She can't really be gone.' Mag crept up the steps, the solid oak steps not creaking even a little. Mag stood to one side of the door, adrenaline coursing through his body at the speed of light preparing him for battle.

He listened. . . No footsteps coming from a distant room, no hushed voices. Mag turned the knob. It was unlocked. 'What if he is sitting in the living room with a gun?' Mag thought. He quietly descended the steps and removed a brick that made up part of a flower bed. His plan was to fling the door open and throw the brick directly at whoever may be holding a weapon and hope for a good enough blow to allow him enough time to rush in.

Mag threw the massive oak door open, brick raised, heart rate raised, nil.

The living room was empty of people, modest ranch décor. High upon the ceiling a wood and gold trimmed ceiling fan silently spun. The horrible stench was coming and going in waves.

The stench and then some kind of chemical cleaning agent were taking turns invading Mag's nose.

The room was spacious and softly lit. Big cats, bears, and huge deer heads adorned the walls. They all seemed to be giving Mag a look that said: GET OUT.

The living room and kitchen were separated by a mini bar. The bar counter was lined with six stools and different liquors were displayed on the shelf behind it. The light was on in the kitchen but it was empty. At the back of the kitchen Mag noticed a door. He guessed it was a bedroom. On the left side of the living room Mag passed a set of stairs that went down he guessed to some type of basement.

He thought that he would wake up at any moment as he slid towards the door with his back against the wall, brick in hand, same plan. Mag listened, nil. He pushed the door open but stayed flat against the outside wall. He figured that the motion of the door flying open would cause a gun wielding person to fire a succession of shots or a knife wielder to maybe throw it.

Mag looked in. It was a bedroom. The bed was carved into Egyptian styled art work. The room smelled of cigars. It was empty. 'Where the hell is she?' Mag came out of the room and set the brick on the kitchen counter. The stench hit him flush in the nose again. 'What the hell is that?' Mag thought, then he heard a voice warn him from within, 'GET OUT BEFORE YOU DIE IN THE TRAP'. Mag fought with his anger back and forth as he headed towards the door. Someone had to pay.

Mag walked through the kitchen and passed the stairs on his right. He got to the front door and paused. . . The stairs. . . Someone had to pay. He couldn't just leave. Yes, the stairs.

CHAPTER 18: VICTOR

The stairs strained under Mag's weight. Whoever had built the steps outside certainly didn't use the same wood on these steps. It got darker and darker the further he got down the steps. The sun outside was now in REM sleep. Mag looked back one last time, the animals on the walls still telling him the same thing.

The whole way down Mag was feeling for a light switch, nil. He was holding onto the rail and feeling each step out as he went. At the bottom he felt around and found a door handle. He waited and listened. Nil, no chainsaw motor, no women screaming, no thumps or bumps. Mag realized that he'd left his brick on the kitchen counter. He'd have to improvise.

Mag turned the handle slowly and pushed open the door. An odor slammed into Mag's nose full force. He dry heaved twice, rage and determination keeping him going. Mag immediately stopped breathing through his nose, a trick he learned in prison after having a cell mate who had bad gas. Mag felt around the inner wall and felt a light switch. He flipped it. The light illuminated another set of steps leading down to a concrete landing. The stench was so bad he could taste it. How anyone could live around it was beyond Mag.

Mag started down the stairs. Something was rotting; maybe a body in the first stages of decomposition, or a fresh deer waiting to be cleaned. Mag recognized the smell from prison. An old man died with his head under the covers in the cell next to him and it took the guards three days to discover that he was dead.

Mag reached the bottom of the steps and realized that he was standing in a makeshift studio. Three lines ran from wall to wall, photos in different stages of development hung on the lines. Mag pulled a string hanging from the ceiling and red light filled the room.

There were long plastic tables on each side of the room with water trays for developing pictures. The first set of pictures confirmed Mag's fears. They were of the girl from the restaurant, Lora. She was getting in her car in the first photo, standing in front of an apartment in another. The next picture made Mag look away for a second. She was naked and sprawled out on the floor in what looked to Mag to be an apartment living room. She was covered in blood. "What the fuck," Mag said, "you sick bitch." Mag remembered the evil in Jasmine's eyes the night she'd hit Lora over the head. Had to stop her from bashing her brains out right in front of everyone. The next pictures were close ups of her hands and feet after the digits had been removed. A crazy time to remember but he remembered that 'digit' was from the Latin word 'digitus', meaning finger, toe, pointer, and derived from the practice of people counting with their fingers and toes.

Mag suppressed the urge to dry heave again. The stench had its own presence in the room. 'Why couldn't I see this in her?' Mag pondered.

The next line of pictures were still drying and they instantly caused tears to flood from Mag's eyes. They were of Stacy parked outside the zoo on their way in, frozen in time forever. Mag remembered feeling like they were being followed. He was right. Stacy was smiling and full of life. The next picture was of them eating on Stacy's back patio, Stacy forever caught in time throwing a green bean at Mag. He smiled as tears tasted like salt on his lips. Someone had to pay. Mag remembered that right after the picture was taken they had made love for the first and last time.

Just a glimpse of the next picture was a blow strong enough to knock the wind out of Mag and drop him to one knee sobbing. The enormous amount of pressure in his chest was about to explode, it was almost too much. "I'm sorry baby," his voice cracked, "I brought this evil upon you, and I'm sorry. If you can hear me please forgive me. I will make this right if it takes the rest of my life for me to do it!"

Mag's burden was fueled by a fury of uncontrollable rage causing him to shoot from his knee and rip the line from the walls. He was ripping and throwing pictures everywhere. The metal water trays crashed to the ground with a clank. Water was everywhere.

From the tables Mag pulled out drawers and dumped the contents on the floor. An envelope landed in a small puddle of water with a thud. Mag opened it.

In the pictures an old Caucasian man was eating dinner with a young Chinese girl. The next picture was of the Caucasian man entering a hotel with the same girl. "Her husband," Mag whispered as tears fell onto the picture he was holding. The next picture showed the man dead in an open field area covered in blood, his digits missing. "Crazy bitch killed her husband too."

Off in the right hand corner of the room Mag noticed a blue waste barrel with a lid. Mag unclipped the metal seal that was holding the lid in place. The stench was so powerful Mag had to cover his mouth and his nose with his shirt. Mag tossed the lid to the side and was horrified.

The barrel was a quarter of the way full of digits in various stages of decomposition. The room all of a sudden started to feel like it was closing in on Mag. Unconsciously he was already backing out of the room. It was unbearable for him to even consider the thought that he was in the same room with Stacy's fingers and toes. The same ones that he'd kissed and caressed just days ago.

Mag's heels hit the bottom of the step. He was dizzy with fury and pain. He turned and sprinted up both sets of stairs. As soon as he reached the top step Victor was coming through the door carrying a large machete.

Mag instantly recognized the Gerber Gator Kukri machete. It was a tool based on a century old design with a pointed tip for piercing, a wide midsection for chopping and a narrow neck for detailed work. The machete was about nineteen inches long with a blade length of about twelve inches from what Mag could tell. It was a merciless weapon with full tang construction, 1050 steel, and a gator grip handle. It was a true multipurpose weapon.

Mag and Victor locked eyes. Mag was winded from the sprint up the stairs and the rampage downstairs. Victor closed the door behind him. Mag walked to the middle of the living room, his back to the mini-bar and kitchen.

Mag said, "I got no real beef with you school, just stay out of my way. Where's Jasmine?"

Victor let out an evil sounding chuckle. He said, "I knew you would be trouble from the start. You mayates always are." His accent was thick and he spoke slow eyeing Mag.

"What do you mean from the start? You don't know me!"

Mag walked behind the bar and poured himself a shot of Grey Goose. He downed the shot to help calm his nerves and hopefully numb the pain. "Drink?"

Victor ignored the drink offer and said, "I know your type and I saw the way she use to obsess over your fucking picture. I knew you would hurt her and I couldn't have that. My brother

Torrez couldn't do the job and now look what the fuck I gots to do Holmes."

Mag came from behind the bar thinking and then it made sense. Victor had sent Torrez to prevent Jasmine from falling for him. He was never supposed to have made it out of prison.

"So you sent your bro to shank me punk?! I promise you won't live to regret that choice, you or your crazy ass daughter." Mag said.

Victor chuckled again as if Mag was telling jokes, "Yeah, my beautiful daughter Jasmine, she has emotional trauma but far from crazy. You got it all wrong homie, and you got life very very confused if you think I'll let you hurt my baby!"

Mag was scanning the room for anything he could arm himself with. If push came to shove the brick in the kitchen would have to do.

Victor continued, "See her husband thought he was smooth too vato," he let out an evil laugh again, "but now he's out back in the wood resting. I did him worse than the vatos in Mexico."

Mag grabbed the bottle of Grey Goose from the bar and acted like he took a swig, a better weapon than any. Mag said nothing, pieces of the puzzle starting to come together. Mag took another swig from the bottle, made it look real. His feelings changed about wanting to kill Victor when he put another piece of the puzzle into perspective for him.

"I've been watching you too," Victor said, "Just like I watched her husband with the Chinese girl. I warned you didn't I? At the restaurant. This is on you, not me. I gave you a chance. I enjoyed the white girl Lora a little too much. She had the nerve to disrespect my princess like that. I made her pay dearly."

A disturbing realization came over Mag at once. Victor was right, he'd had it wrong all along. 'This crazy son of a bitch was behind the madness the whole time. Stacy! What about Stacy?'

Victor must of read Mag's mind or the tears in his eyes, "And that silky smooth negrita girl, I tracked the phone Jasmine gave you to find her house. I couldn't resist her body. I had to have some. Then I made her pay too. My princess deserves what she wants and she was in the way!"

Mag erupted with savage fury, throwing the Grey Goose bottle at Victor with brutal strength. The bottle shot through the air and exploded against Victor's right shoulder, glass and liquor flying to the floor. The impact made Victor drop the machete, but he retrieved it just as fast as he'd dropped it. Victor was holding his right shoulder with his left hand.

"You broke my fucking collar bone puta. I'll cut you to pieces."

Mag removed his shirt and wrapped it around his left arm as a shield. They moved in circles around the room. Mag was looking for anything, something to use as a weapon. Victor swung at Mag's head and Mag ducked and hit Victor in his right knee with a right hook. Mag felt the knee slightly give then stabilize. Prison had prepared Mag for these types of encounters. Victor thrust the machete at Mag's stomach causing Mag's head to come forward. Victor hit Mag with a flush left cross. Victor followed the blow by coming over the top with the machete. Mag blocked it with his left arm and hit Victor with a vicious right elbow to the jaw. Victor staggered back and spit out blood. Mag rushed in and Victor slashed Mag's left arm. Blood began to ooze from the wound. Mag staggered back, willing himself to stay focused.

Victor's right shoulder must've been in pain because he switched the machete to his left hand. Mag's power leg was his right even though he could use both sides of his body. Mag threw a right cross kick and it landed flush on Victor's left wrist sending the knife flying across the room.

Mano-e-mano, just the way Mag wanted it. Victor threw an overhand faster than Mag expected and it caught Mag at the top of his left eye. The blow split Mag's eyebrow and blood began to run into his eye. Mag attempted to wipe as much of the blood as he could while staying focused. Mag threw a left jab followed with a mighty right jab that busted Victor's nose. Blood was pouring from Victor's nose and he was licking it from his lips and smiling.

Mag realized real fast that the old man was no pushover. They were back to moving in circles.

Victor reached down on the table and grabbed something and threw it hard at Mag. It was one of those balls you shake up and snow goes all over before it settles back at the bottom. Mag tried to dodge it but it struck with thunderous impact right between his eyes. Mag fell to his knees, his vision blurry, disoriented. A second later Victor kicked Mag in the side of the head. Mag fell to his side and rolled to his back fighting unconsciousness.

Victor was walking around Mag in circles, blood still leaking from his nose. He said, "I told you but you wouldn't listen," Victor kicked Mag in the ribs. "I'm going to enjoy cutting you up into little pieces." Victor made chopping motions with his hands into his other one. "I'll tie you up and cut off your fingers then your toes while you are awake!"

Mag was fighting to come back from the fogginess knowing that his life depended on it. He was using Stacy's vengeance as fuel. As soon as his head started to clear up and the fogginess started to leave Mag felt a weight on him and two hands around his neck.

Victor spit the words at Mag, "No! I'll kill you now and look deep into your eyes as the life flows from them."

Mag was going back out, back into the darkness, when he heard a voice from a distance place say, "Dad, no!" Victor looked behind him towards the door. It was the break Mag needed. Mag rolled his body hard to the left as hard as he could and mounted Victor. He threw the hardest elbow he could muster, everything he had. It got the job done. The force of the blow crushed Victor's wind pipe, destroying his trachea and cutting off the air supply to his lungs. Victor's nose was already clogged. Mag followed the blow with two more explosive elbows. He said, "That's for Stacy, bitch!" He rolled off Victor to his left trying to find his equilibrium.

Victor was making all kinds of choking sounds while holding his throat. His eyes were red and moving from side to side. Jasmine was at his side rubbing his arm in a soothing manner, tears sprinting down her face leaving trails. The choking sound stopped and Victor went limp.

She ran over to Mag, "What the hell Mag, I don't understand. My father is dead. What did you do? Why?" She was pulling at Mag's shirt, one that she had bought.

She was hysterical. Blood was everywhere. Mag was pointing at the stairs trying to get his mouth to speak the words his mind wanted to convey, "Down, down there, go, go see for yourself," Mag whispered as he filled his lungs with every ounce of air he could get.

Mag looked over at Victor. His eyes were still open but the absent stare told their secret: they were void of life.

CHAPTER 19: SOLDIER

Ten long minutes later when Jasmine came back from the basement Mag had finished two shots of Crown Royal to clear the cobwebs and was now sitting at the bar drinking a cold glass of water; Exasperated, numb, fully understanding now the implications of the trap. He'd cleaned his arm and eye up as best he could. The bleeding has stopped in both wounds.

From the corner of his eye he saw Jasmine walking towards him coming from the basement. She sat down next to him and poured her own shot of Crown. They sat quiet for a long time both contemplating the images that would be seared into their minds-eye forever. Mag had pulled the blanket from Victor's bed and used it to cover him up. Tears rolled down her face as she stared at his body wrapped on the floor.

Her voice cracked, "I'm so sorry Mag. I, I didn't know," she cried, "I didn't know he was behind it all. I swear I didn't know. You have to believe me Mag."

He raised a hand indicating that it was okay, "Come here, come here," he held her as she cried. "It's me that owes you an apology. I read the signs wrong and thought it was you. I'm so sorry." The idea of revealing what he knew about her obsession with him from his profile entered his mind. He decided against it. He just wanted to go. Even though Victor was gone it did nothing to ease the grief he felt about Stacy.

He said, "Listen to me carefully Jasmine. I WAS NEVER HERE!" He was looking deep into her eyes making sure she knew he was serious. "I never got into that car with you that day. You don't know a man named Ty Magnum, ok?"

"You're leaving me?" She asked almost in disbelief, "None of this is my fault Mag. We can make it go away. I love you. I don't care about the girl in the pictures down there!"

"Am I leaving!" Mag just looked at her with a dumbfounded look on his face and ignored the question.

Mag stood. He realized that his blood and fingerprints were all over the place. "We have to burn this cabin down and everything in it. I need you to go find some gas and matches. Cover this place in as much gas as possible and burn it to the ground. I'm going out back to burry your father's body. This way he will always be near you. Ok? Go!"

Jasmine had fear and sorrow in her eyes. Her hands were shaking, but she slowly nodded her head and walked off.

Outside Mag was thinking of every angle he needed to focus on to cover his tracks. He would make sure that if police leads lead to Jasmine and they asked about 'the black guy' whom you were seen at the restaurant with that she answered 'a guy from a dating app whom gave me a false name, it didn't work out'. Mag wondered if he had left any prints inside of Jasmine's house that lead to him, if his DNA was left on her bedroom covers and investigations lead his way he would deal with it then.

He threw Victor's body over Queen. She stirred under his weight but all was necessary for him not to end up back in the stir. "It's okay girl, this won't take us long, I got you."

In the shed Mag found a shovel and rode off into the woods. The ground was hard and the work was grueling but Eleanor Roosevelt once said, "What one has to do, usually can be done." Mag agreed.

Mag smelled smoke riding on the wind, a black cloud rose and was camouflaged by the night. When he got back to the cabin Jasmine was standing outside with a gas can looking lost in the flames. Mag rode up behind her and took in the scene. Flames danced in and out of the windows playing peek-a-boo. Mag could feel the heat from where he was standing.

"Let's go," he said.

Jasmine jumped on the back of Queen and they rode to the main house. Mag jumped off the horse and sprinted through the kitchen and up the stairs to his room. He pulled the suitcase from the closet and chose a fresh set of clothes, socks, and boxers. The shower took him five minutes, ten minutes he was back fully dressed.

Mag took a rag and wiped the room down as much as he could. He did the same with the bathroom, Jasmine's room, and her remote. He put his watch and ring in the top zipper of the suitcase along with the camera from the zoo, the only piece of Stacy he had left besides his memories.

Jasmine was coming in the front door as he came off the bottom step, tears falling from her eyes, her mascara running.

Mag broke the silence, "Jasmine remember everything that I told you. This moment is the beginning of the rest of your life. Our road may be ending but your life is beginning."

She said, her eyes filled with a strange pain, it was as if it was a part of her eyes. In that moment Mag knew the truth of eyes being the window to one's soul; "thank you for, for trying. I will carry your words with me. I, I left you a gift in your car. It's a token of my appreciation for everything Mag. I will love you forever."

Jasmine smiled a weak smile, took the gun from the back of her waistband and shot herself in the temple! POW! The pearl handled twenty five sounded like a bomb in Mag's mind.

Mag stood with his mouth wide open, frozen in shock, horrified. He reached a shaky hand out towards her lifeless body. He pulled it back speechless. Mag cried for her as he walked around her crumpled body. He cried for the little girl that never healed. He cried for not having the healing words that could have saved her.

His heart and mind were so heavy it was as if he was walking in slow motion, a fog of disbelief. He had to wake up soon, he had to. The sorrow was so heavy in his heart he couldn't take in the beauty of his new car. Mag threw his luggage into the back seat and wiped a solo tear from his eye as he tried to steady his soul.

The keys were under the sun visor as instructed. The car started with a deep growl then leveled out. Mag pulled out and it took no time before he was floating down a highway he had no name for. He just drove. At the top of the highway he could see the Alamo lit up in the distance. He regretted not having the chance to set foot on the historic ground where so many brave men had given their lives for Texas.

It seemed the further he got away from the city the better he felt. When his mind cleared he noticed that he was on I-35 North. He passed a sign saying that he had entered Universal City's city limits. He ate up more highway and the next sign he noticed said he was now in a place called New Braunfels.

Even though he felt he'd prepared himself mentally for the challenges of the free world, he had to admit that he had some mental weaknesses that were dangerous to his success.

As he sailed the highway the night air turned his tears into white streaks on his face. He was all cried out, he knew it, now came the journey of not forgetting what he had been through, but finding a way to remember without the pain and taking the lessons forward.

The Cadillac ate the highway lines up like pac-man as Mag thought about waking up one night as a boy: He'd been sleeping on a pallet in the living room when the familiar snap of a mouse trap pulled him from his dreams. Mag remembered hearing the mouse struggling in the trap and decided to take a look. Mag turned on the kitchen light and roaches ran for cover. A few stayed to cheer on the mouse.

The mouse's tail was pinned down by the trap. He'd been blessed, the bar had missed his body by an inch. Mag noticed that the mouse had managed to bend his tail backwards and drag the trap across the tile floor until he'd reached the carpet in the living room. The trap was hung on the edge of the carpet. Mag noticed that the mouse was smart and was using it as leverage.

"Come on little fella, you can do it. Keep pulling, keep moving, you're almost there." Young Mag remembered saying, pumping his fist at the mouse.

He seemed to respond to Mag's encouragement or either he was spooked by Mag's voice. Whatever his motivation the mouse pulled harder, gripping the carpet with his claws, his tail began to give way from the trap a little at a time.

"That's it, that's it, you're almost there, keep pulling."

The mouse pulled hard one last time with all his might and finally his tail slipped from the trap.

Mag exploded with excitement, "Yeah! YOU DID IT!" he was clapping as the mouse gathered himself and scampered off.

"Boy what all that racket in there? Take yo ass to sleep in there before I come in there and help you," his grandfather said from his bedroom.

"Yes sir," Mag had a smile on his face and decided to give the mouse his own name: Soldier. After that Mag had started to sneak and put little bits of cheese inside the pantry for him.

The highway stole Mag's consciousness back from the past and Mag realized he had been blessed like his boy Soldier by the mere fact that when the trap had snapped, it had missed his life by an inch; and because of his determination to fight, he had survived. He wondered if life would sneak him bits of cheese moving forward.

Chapter 20: Stace

The sun was starting to stretch his body getting ready to start its morning as Mag passed through San Marcos, then Kyle, and finally he passed a sign that said that he had entered Austin city limits, the state capitol. Mag took an exit promising food and accommodations. He pulled into a Taco Bell and ordered a double decker and a sprite.

Down the street Mag entered Wal-Mart and was amazed at the number of items that were available in one spot. A few women gave him eyes that said, 'damn you fine', but his mind was a million miles away. He took his camera to the picture developing station and offered the Hispanic lady 'extra' for speedy service. She leaned in and told Mag for $30 she could have them ready in less than twenty minutes.

Mag wasted the time buying hygiene items, microwavable pizzas, and a first aid kit to treat his wounds. He grabbed a few envelopes and some stamps along with the pictures on his way out. He felt as if he was walking in a fog. He was tired, his body beckoning for rest, for sleep.

He pulled into the Motel 6 parking lot, turned his car off and sighed. His choices and decisions had cost lives. He had ignored wisdom at every turn. What were the lessons? Blame would only cripple him. He would take the lessons and move on.

A flash of Jasmine's body hitting the floor shot through his mind. He shook the image, then heard her voice in his head, "I left you a token of my appreciation in your car. . ."

Mag scanned the car and didn't notice anything in the passenger seat or floorboard. He bent over and hit the latch for the glove department, nil. He looked over into the back seat, nil except for his suitcase. Mag hit the bottom for the trunk, walked around to the back of the car. There was nothing in the trunk. He lifted the grey rug material and was looking at an extra 24' Assassin rim and a car jack. Mag closed the trunk and walked into the lobby and came out with a key for a single bedroom. Mag thought about leaving the top down on his car but didn't know the neighborhood so decided against it. Before closing the driver's side door he noticed something tucked under the seat. He could see a piece of it from the side. What he pulled from under the seat was wrapped in solid gold paper. 'To: Mag' was written on top. Mag shook the box. The contents shifted to the left and then to the right. Solid, whatever it was. The package weighed five pounds easy, if not more. Mag tucked the box under his arm, grabbed his bag and entered his room.

The room was nowhere near the elegance of his last room but it was good enough for how he was feeling. As soon as his body hit the mattress he was out.

Mag woke the next morning with a start, the knock on his door had been the SNAP of a trap in his dream; it all came back to him as he looked through the peephole hoping the police weren't waiting to ask him what seemed to be their favorite question, "What were you doing the last twenty four hours?"

It was the house keeping lady. Mag pulled the door until the chain caught, the bright sunlight made him squint. "Check out time," the small Latin woman said. Mag held up one finger and came back with a twenty dollar bill. He held it through the opening.

"Come back in a couple of hours and I'll be gone. You got my word." Mag said.

The lady looked to her left and then her right. She took the bill, stuffed it in her bra and walked off.

The room was stuffy so Mag turned the air on. It didn't take long for it to cool. He took a long shower allowing the warm water to soothe the aches and pains on his body. In the mirror Mag noticed that his left eye was slightly swollen but nothing too serious. He bandaged the slash on his arm and dressed.

He put a pizza in the microwave and noticed the box with the gold wrapping laying on the table. He sat down and undid the wrapper. He lifted the lid and his mouth dropped and his eyes opened an inch more. The box was filled to the rim with stacks of hundred dollar bills. Mag estimated about twenty separate stacks. Each stack had a band around it that contained the number $5,000.

There was a letter folded on top of the money:

Ty,

if you're reading this you're gone from my life and I'm gone from life too. Please don't blame yourself. I'm just tired. Before you got out of prison I vowed that if you wouldn't love me then I didn't want to live. Ty, take this $100,000 as a small token of everything I know you blessed me with while you were a part of my life. Live life to the fullest and never forget, I love you.

Love,

Jasmine

Mag put the lid back on the box feeling a weight lift from his shoulders and his soul. 'She had planned from the beginning everything, even her death! There was nothing I could have done or said to save her besides staying with her forever, which was out of the question.'

The ding from the microwave pulled Mag from his thoughts. As he ate he flipped through the pictures of him and Stacy and smiled. He fought tears because he had made a conscious decision to be thankful for the time that he was blessed to spend with her instead of living in regret of the time he didn't. Blame would only kill that memory.

Mag flipped through his phone and downloaded the JPay app. He put in his boy Santana's information and wrote him.

What's good bro? told you that I would never forget about you. I just shot you $300 to your books and I'll be setting the phone up soon too. Bro, I can't give you the details in writing (we'll talk at visit) but pray for ya boy. I really need it. I just learned that I wasn't as ready for the world as I thought I was and that as we walk through this life we must never not be lead by the Spirit. Do 'you' if you want to!

Winston Churchill once said, "Face adversity without flinching and you'll reduce its impact." This is my attempt at the moment bro. James Allen wrote in his book 'As A Man Thinketh', "People are anxious to improve their circumstances but are unwilling to improve themselves; they therefore remain bound." Bro, I found both of these quotes to be true in this last week! Try as you may you can't save everyone. I found out that some things from my childhood such as poverty still affect some of the choices and risks I'm willing to take. I'm gone be alright bro, no need to worry.

Overall, looking back from my childhood traumas, all the times I almost lost my life in prison, and what I just survived the last week, I have no choice but to believe that God's grace is real.

P.S. Even though life is full of struggles and trials, here are a few pictures to verify that life is also full of blessings. (Yeah, I know) Smile. I'm sending color pics via snail mail.

Ya Boy,
Mag

Mag sealed and addressed the envelope, gathered his things, and realized that he felt rested but sore. He slipped five one hundred dollar bills into his pocket, took one last look at the room and slipped out into the July 2nd sun. His Rolex said that it was 2:00 PM and the air was warm and humid.

Mag threw his bags into the trunk and noticed a man nearby bending down slapping a dog over and over again. He was yelling something that was not audible. Mag could tell by the dog's energy that it was not good. Mag closed his trunk and walked over.

Trying to use tact Mag said, "What's going on pal?"

"Oh nothing, trying to get this little bitch to shit so that I can get the hell out of this sun. The little BITCH getting on my last nerves!" The man yelled bitch at the dog when he said it.

The dog looked up at Mag. They locked eyes. Mag knew it that moment that nothing could stop him from taking the dog with him. Mag noticed the rubber band tight around the dog's tail, cutting off its circulation. Its ears were in bad shape also. They looked like someone had taken a razor and had tried to make the ears pointy. It looked like they gave up after the dog wouldn't be still. The dog was a malnutritioned Doberman Pincher about four months old.

The slob raised his hand to hit the dog again and Mag caught his wrist in mid swing, anger in his eyes, a dangerous anger coming from a place of pain.

"Heeey, let my arm go! Who do you think you are man?" Mag heard a quiver in the man's voice. The dog was looking at Mag, curious with a look that had hope.

"I'm going to make you a deal you can't refuse," Mag said, "I can kick your mutha-fuckin ass right here right now and take her, or I can give you $300 cash right now on the spot, right now, and you no longer have a problem on your hands that's causing 'shit', your choice."

The guy swallowed hard, looked down at the dog and back up at Mag, "$300 for this bitch? You got yourself a deal. Where my money?"

Mag handed the slob the bills and the slob gave Mag the leash. "Let's go girl," Mag said. She followed Mag without one moment's hesitation.

Mag picked her up and put her in his passenger seat and walked around to get in the driver's seat. He immediately let the top down. He raised his hand to pet the dog and she flinched but then let Mag rub her head. She licked his hand before he pulled it back.

He said, "It's okay Stace, you'll learn you can trust me. Let's get you to the vet and then we'll see what Austin, Texas has to offer."

THE END

Preview of "Escaping the Pen"

You come across our title: Escaping the Pen, and you are intrigued. You flip the book over and discover that this is not some book about a couple of offenders who dug a three-hundred-foot tunnel to freedom, but about two men in prison who dug into themselves and did the hard work of soul searching in order to gain the true meaning of freedom.

Then you scratch your head and a small question enters your mind-why should I listen to someone in prison? I am out here in society as a productive member. What can someone in prison teach me? Well, I'm glad you asked.

First, I would like to point out something that a lot of people simply fail to take into account--part of one of the most prolific books of all time was written in a prison. It's one of the top-selling books of all time and has inspired some of the greatest transformations the world has ever seen. Maybe you've already guessed it, The Holy Bible.

Paul, while in the solitude of his cell, wrote a big portion of the New Testament. He could have easily written these pages in the free society where a wealth of materials was at his disposal, or even the best of scribes who would have offered their services to such a great man. Ralph Walden Emerson once said, 'When it is dark enough, you can see the stars." We can imagine Paul in his darkest moment finally finding the words within his Soul that were meant for the world, connecting with his purpose and deciding to share it with the world. We don't have to imagine because the book that you are now reading was forged in the same type of darkness and we now share our souls with the world.

Another great leader who rose from the grime of the street and entered the prison system also left a lasting legacy after his incarceration: Malcom X (1925-1965). He was known as 'Detroit Red' in the streets. He entered the prison system just as many other young black men before him, stuck in the cycle of the system. With a lack of distraction bombarding his mind and heart, looking for something different, Malcom began a journey in prison that would impact an entire culture and influence many great young leaders for generations to come. It seems as if in the streets, Malcom was incarcerated mentally in a cycle of destruction that kept him enslaved. But, through the darkness and solitude of prison, he was able to connect with what he was destined for. We understand the solitude and darkness of prison can be turned into a tool that liberates the soul and sets your life on a course of true destiny. We understand because this is our journey and just as a farmer takes dung and turns it into a tool of growth, we have learned this secret and, in this book, we share it with you for your life.

The last two historical figures we used as examples we never got to meet, even though their life has touched ours. Our brother and close friend, Ryan Moody, who graciously wrote the forward, is a living witness to what it means to 'escape the pen.' We will get deeper into the particular details of his story later in the book, but when you enter Moody's presence you can feel his spiritual, mental, and emotional power. Despite his potential incarceration for life, he has mastered the art of being free internally. He is a living witness of how prison can be used as a tool of true liberation and how those lessons can be passed on to others. Everywhere he goes he takes his freedom with him and does his best to live this truth. We know the principles that we are about to share can change your life and set you free because our minds and hearts have been transformed; we are just saving you a prison trip. You're welcome. :)

If handing you lessons that we had to gain through hard time isn't enough motivation for you, we would like to add that combined, we have over twenty years of 'doing' time and not just 'passing' it.

On a daily basis, it is not hard to encounter a man or woman in society or prison who, when you ask 'what's up?' responds, "just maintaining," "just tryna make it," or "passing time, bro." Most of these individuals, if you had a chance to watch them for a day, you would see them just going through the motions without passion or direction. See, to us, 'passing time' is passive. A common definition of passive is, "accepting what happens without resisting or trying to change anything." People like this are slaves to the system and blindly follow the path that is laid out for them to follow. We see it here in prison everyday where TV, games, drugs, and 'penitentiary games,' are used as devices to distract individuals from taking responsibility for the outcomes of their lives.

'Doing' is a verb. It requires action. A person doing their time is actively executing the vision they have set forth for themselves and not just following or accepting what comes. So, when we say that we have been doing time, we are essentially saying that you can trust that we have been doing our time, we are essentially saying that you can trust the principles that we are about share because what you now hold in your hands is evidence that though our bodies are locked up, our minds have found the true keys to liberation. We have used our incarceration as a tool to find our way out of the internal limits that have held us back for so long.

Not only is the book that you are now reading evidence of our mentality of 'doing' our time, but between the both of us, we have college degrees and over twenty plus years of life skills, courses, and trades that we have capitalized on here in prison.

Combined, we have read well over five hundred fiction and non-fiction titles such as Think and Grow Rich, Mastery, The Road Less Travelled, etc.

We are both very passionate about fitness and have transformed our bodies by adding an average of twenty pounds of muscle to the frames that we came into prison with. We are workout partners and we push each other daily to be diligent about today and not using yesterday as an excuse to slack.

Spiritually we are both still growing and evolving and we have a healthy appreciation for the Creator who gave us this world filled with possibilities.

Each day we plant seeds mentally, physically, and spiritually. In a days' time, if an individual would 'do' something that contributed to his mental sharpness and growth, if he would stimulate his body in a way that reduced stress and improved overall health, and walk in constant appreciation spiritually-aware and connected to his creator; this individual would know the difference between just being alive and actually living.

Yes, we know these truths, but the sad reality is that a countless number of people are trapped and stuck behind mental and emotional walls and can't find the keys of release. James Allen said it this way: "People are anxious to improve their circumstances but are unwilling to improve themselves, they are therefore bound." My coauthor, Buddy, says it this way: "No one can give you freedom; freedom comes when you open your mind."

We find people from all walks of life, different cultures, and socioeconomic backgrounds blame their environments, relationships, and jobs for the 'caged' conditions that control the direction and energy of their lives. The truth is that it's never our circumstances that enslaves us. Dr. M. Scott Peck, M.D. said that a lot of people use external things and people to "escape from freedom," in essence to give responsibility over to something outside ourselves. Dr. Peck said, "The difficulty we have in accepting responsibility for our behavior lies in the desire to avoid the pain of the consequences of that behavior."

What has so many people internally incarcerated is not the condition of their lives, but the condition of their minds. Throughout this book we will share with you how, despite being locked in a physical prison, we escaped into ourselves and now have a strong desire to share our freedom with you in hope that your cages will also open within. It's our desire to show you the keys that already lie waiting inside you that confine you. In the end, it's our hope that you will know and understand and then apply through wisdom, the truth that no circumstance can enslave you when your mind is free.

You are about to go on a fifteen-year journey of growth with us. During this journey of enlightenment, we will highlight unique aspects of prison life we used as tools to set our minds free and transform our lives.

We will touch on unique aspects from prison such as the intake/line class system and how it is related to the systems we start off in out in society that can seem to confine us to the perceived limitations of those starting points in life.

We will highlight the cell and how it is designed as a place of confinement and restraint, a place that is dark and meant to keep you from the light. This place can actually be used as a place of growth and development, a place for soul-searching to find the keys to your freedom. In the "Keys to Freedom" at the end of each chapter, Buddy will write and give you keys from his perspective that cap off the chapter.

You have just been sentenced to "do" fifteen years, my friend. We see potential in you and have decided to take you under our wing and "lace you up" on the ins and outs of prison life and how to maximize and "do" your time, not allowing it to do you. "Let's Ride!"

MOUSE TRAP

About the Author

Through the early traumatic event of his mother surviving being shot by his father, KING-B learned the power of how pain can be transformed for good or bad. He used the pain and discomfort of prison life to transform his mind and the mind of others who didn't know the power of pain. In his co-authored book Escaping the Pen, he teaches how to escape 'inner' prisons; in his first fiction Mouse Trap he shows the tragic consequences of these prisons. KING B is from Wichita Falls, Texas and is a Life Coach and Motivational Speaker.

www.ingramcontent.com/pod-product-compliance
Lightning Source LLC
Chambersburg PA
CBHW070549100726

47907CB00004B/1319